① Feb 9 2018

OCT 17 201

W9-BNB-411

"Long time no see, Curtis."

He was about to reply when she came closer and the words evaporated on his tongue.

Barrie's tan canvas winter coat was open in the front, and her belly swelled under a loose cream-colored sweater. She sauntered down the aisle toward him, her vet bag slung over one shoulder, and stopped at the stall.

"You're—" He wasn't sure if he was allowed to point out the obvious, but he'd never been a terribly diplomatic guy. "You're pregnant."

"I am." She met his gaze evenly.

"Congratulations." He wasn't sure what else to say. Somehow, in all of his considerations surrounding seeing Barrie again, he hadn't considered this one.

"Thank you." For the first time, her confidence seemed to falter, and color rose in her cheeks. "You look good, Curtis."

His jeans were mud smeared and he hadn't shaved in several days, but he'd take the compliment. He allowed himself one more glance down her figure before he locked his gaze firmly on her face and kept it there. Her body, and her baby, weren't his business.

Dear Reader,

Christmas isn't always an easy time of year, but it comes around whether we're ready for it or not. I'm glad that Christmas comes relentlessly, because I think we need the sparkle. The holidays force us to look up—to the lights, to the decorations and to the people around us. We're never as alone as we think. I hope this Christmas is a happy one for you, and that you're able to find some of that Christmas magic.

If you enjoyed this book and my other Hope, Montana stories, you might also want to check out my books in the Love Inspired and Heartwarming lines. I have a feeling you might like them. If you'd like to connect with me, you can find me on Facebook or at my website, patriciajohnsromance.com.

A very merry Christmas from my home to yours!

Patricia Johns

MONTANA
MISTLETOE BABY

———

PATRICIA JOHNS

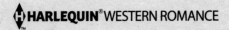
HARLEQUIN® WESTERN ROMANCE

If you purchased this book without a cover you should be aware that this book is stolen property. It was reported as "unsold and destroyed" to the publisher, and neither the author nor the publisher has received any payment for this "stripped book."

Recycling programs
for this product may
not exist in your area.

ISBN-13: 978-0-373-75788-6

Montana Mistletoe Baby

Copyright © 2017 by Patricia Johns

All rights reserved. Except for use in any review, the reproduction or utilization of this work in whole or in part in any form by any electronic, mechanical or other means, now known or hereinafter invented, including xerography, photocopying and recording, or in any information storage or retrieval system, is forbidden without the written permission of the publisher, Harlequin Enterprises Limited, 225 Duncan Mill Road, Don Mills, Ontario M3B 3K9, Canada.

This is a work of fiction. Names, characters, places and incidents are either the product of the author's imagination or are used fictitiously, and any resemblance to actual persons, living or dead, business establishments, events or locales is entirely coincidental.

This edition published by arrangement with Harlequin Books S.A.

For questions and comments about the quality of this book, please contact us at CustomerService@Harlequin.com.

® and TM are trademarks of Harlequin Enterprises Limited or its corporate affiliates. Trademarks indicated with ® are registered in the United States Patent and Trademark Office, the Canadian Intellectual Property Office and in other countries.

Printed in U.S.A.

Patricia Johns writes from Alberta, Canada. She has her Hon. BA in English literature and currently writes for Harlequin's Love Inspired, Western Romance and Heartwarming lines. You can find her at patriciajohnsromance.com.

Books by Patricia Johns

Harlequin Western Romance

Hope, Montana

Safe in the Lawman's Arms
Her Stubborn Cowboy
The Cowboy's Christmas Bride
The Cowboy's Valentine Bride
The Triplets' Cowboy Daddy
Her Cowboy Boss

Harlequin Love Inspired

Comfort Creek Lawmen

His Unexpected Family
The Rancher's City Girl
A Firefighter's Promise
The Lawman's Surprise Family
Deputy Daddy

Harlequin Heartwarming

A Baxter's Redemption
The Runaway Bride
A Boy's Christmas Wish

Visit the Author Profile page at Harlequin.com for more titles.

Chapter One

Curtis Porter was too old to be a bull rider, and right about now, he felt like a failure at ranching, too. When he'd moved away from Hope, Montana, for good, he'd left behind a soon-to-be ex-wife and a whole heap of memories. He figured if he ever came back, he'd show her just what she missed out on. He didn't count on coming back washed up.

Curtis hunkered down next to the calf in the barn stall. The calf was having difficulty breathing and looked thin. It obviously hadn't been eating properly. Curtis had been back on the ranch only since Friday, so he couldn't blame himself for not noticing sooner. Bovine illness could be hard to spot at first glance, but the later stages were obvious. He still wished he hadn't missed this one—he hated the unnecessary suffering.

December was a tough month—the days being snipped shorter and shorter, and darkness stretching out well into his work hours. He did chores in the morning and evening with a flashlight while winter wind buffeted him from all directions. It wasn't an excuse to have missed a sick calf, but it factored in.

Curtis rose to his feet and let himself out of the stall. He'd just have to wait for the vet. He was officially out of his depth. Curtis was a recently retired bull rider, and when the aunt who'd taken him in as a teen asked him to come back to help run the ranch while she recovered from a broken ankle, he'd agreed, but it wasn't only because of his soft spot for Aunt Betty. He had other business to attend to in the tiny town of Hope—the sale of a commercial property—and he'd been putting that off for longer than his finances would comfortably allow. He no longer had the choice—he needed the money now.

Curtis's cell phone blipped, and he looked down at an incoming text from Aunt Betty.

The vet passed the house a couple of minutes ago. Should be there any second.

There was a pause, and then another text came through.

Tried to get Palmer, but he's out at an emergency for the night. Had to call Barrie. Sorry, kiddo.

His heart sped up, and Curtis dropped the phone back into his front pocket. Of course. There were only two vets in Hope, and his ex-wife, Barrie Jones, was one of them. At least Aunt Betty had *tried* for the less awkward option.

The barn door creaked open, and Curtis looked up to see Barrie framed in the doorway. From this vantage point, he could see her only from her shoulders up—chestnut-brown hair pulled back into a ponytail, no makeup and clear blue eyes—and his heart clenched in his chest. Her gaze swept across the barn, then landed on him, pinning him to the spot. Fifteen years, and she could still do that to him.

"Betty said I'd find you out here," Barrie said, pulling the door shut behind her. The sound of her stomping the snow off her boots on concrete echoed through the barn. Then she headed past some stalls toward him. "Long time no see, Curtis."

Apparently Aunt Betty had given Barrie time to compose herself, too. He swallowed hard and was about to reply when she came around to the aisle and the words evaporated on his tongue.

Barrie's tan canvas winter coat was open in the front, and her belly swelled under a loose cream-colored sweater. Her walk was different—more cautious, maybe—but other than the belly, she was still the long-legged beauty she'd always been. Barrie sauntered down the aisle toward him, her vet bag slung over one shoulder. She stopped at the stall.

"You're—" He wasn't sure if he was allowed to point out the obvious, but he'd never been a terribly diplomatic guy. "You're pregnant."

"I am." She met his gaze evenly.

"Congratulations." He wasn't sure what else to say. Somehow, in all of his considerations surrounding seeing Barrie again, he hadn't considered this one.

"Thank you." For the first time, her confidence seemed to falter, and color rose in her cheeks. "You look good, Curtis."

His jeans were mud smeared and he hadn't shaved in several days, but he'd take the compliment. He allowed himself one more glance down her figure before he locked his gaze firmly on her face and kept it there. Her body—and her baby—weren't his business.

"You look good, too," he said. "You're doing really well, then. Your veterinary practice, a baby on the way... So, who's the lucky SOB? Anyone I know?"

It was annoying to admit it, but that was his biggest question right now—who'd managed to make her happy? He couldn't say that he wouldn't be a tiny bit jealous. A man didn't marry a girl, vow to love her until death parted them and then watch her move on with some other guy without at least a twinge of regret.

"I doubt it." Her smile slipped, and she turned toward the stall. "Is this the calf?"

So she wasn't going to tell him? How bad could it be? This only made him all the more curious. He unhinged the latch and opened the gate.

"Seriously?" he asked. "All I have to do is ask Betty who you're with—"

"I'm single." She shot him a sharp look, then went into the stall and crouched down next to the calf. "I'll take a look."

Single? So, some idiot had knocked her up and walked out on her? That sparked some anger deep inside him. He'd walked out, but only after she'd shown him the door, and she most definitely wasn't pregnant when he'd left. So he might be an SOB, too, but whoever had left her alone with this baby was higher on that list.

Barrie put on some rubber gloves, pulled a flashlight

out of her bag and checked the calf's eyes. Then she pulled out a thermometer and murmured reassuringly to the calf as she worked.

"So who's the father?" Curtis pressed.

Barrie glanced up again, then sighed. "Curtis, I'm here to do a job. Would you like to know what's wrong with this calf or not?"

"Fine." He leaned against the rail and watched her check the calf's temperature.

She looked at the readout on the digital recorder. "A cow's body temperature rises continuously during the day, so it's hard to get a really accurate idea of how much fever a calf is running…"

Barrie pulled the plastic cover off the thermometer wand, then dropped it back into her bag. She rose to her feet and turned to Curtis. "But this calf is definitely running a fever. I'm thinking it's probably bovine respiratory disease. It's catchy, so keep an eye on the other calves bought at the same time. It can be transferred to adult cattle, as well, so make sure you quarantine the sick ones or you'll end up with a costly epidemic."

"Got it." He nodded. "Treatment?"

"I'll give antibiotic doses for a few days. It's caused by a virus, but the antibiotics treat any secondary illnesses that develop as a result and let the body focus on fighting the virus. If we find the sick cows early enough, they get over it. If not, it turns into pneumonia and you'll lose them." Barrie opened her bag again and pulled out some packaged cattle syringes and bottles of liquid medication.

She was beautiful when she was focused like that.

Barrie had always been that way—she could be knee-deep in manure and still look sweet. Curtis cared about the cattle—and about the running of his aunt's ranch—but right now, his mind was still working over the fact that Barrie was both single and pregnant. She'd always been the prim and proper type—so much so that it had driven him kind of crazy—so he knew how hard this would be on her.

"Tell me that you told the father to take a hike, and I'll feel better," he said after a moment.

"I don't need defending, Curtis," she replied. "Least of all from the man who walked out on me."

"You kicked me out," he countered.

"And you *left*." Anger snapped in that blue gaze. Then she shook her head. "This is dumb. It was fifteen years ago. There's no use fighting over it."

She had a point. Their relationship was solidly in the past, and whatever her problems now, at least she wasn't blaming him.

"So, how long are you in town?" she asked, turning to the calf again with a syringe. He wasn't sure if she was asking to see how fast she'd be rid of him, or if this was just small talk.

"For a few weeks to help Betty until her ankle heals," he said.

"I'm sure she appreciates it."

"Yeah…" He cleared his throat. Her current state made his other news that much harder to deliver because he'd be the bad guy yet again. But he'd have to tell her eventually. There was no avoiding this one, even if he wanted to.

Barrie administered the syringe, then stroked a hand over the calf's muzzle comfortingly.

"Poor thing," she murmured.

"Will it be okay?" he asked.

"We'll see," she replied. "You may have caught the symptoms in time."

She tried to stand but stumbled. Curtis stepped forward and caught her arm, helping her up.

"I'm fine." She pulled back, and he felt stung. He'd reacted on instinct—she was a pregnant woman, after all, and any able-bodied man would want to give her a hand.

"Look, Barrie, I'm here for something else, too," he admitted.

Barrie's clear blue eyes met his, one eyebrow arched expectantly. She was so close that he could smell the soft scent of her perfume mingling with the tang of other barn aromas. She looked the same—the big blue eyes, the light eyebrows she always used to complain about, the faint spattering of freckles over her nose. Fifteen years had gone by, aging him beyond his ability to keep bull riding, and she still looked as fresh as the twenty-year-old he'd married. He really wished he could have come back a little more successful to prove that she'd missed out, but he couldn't change facts.

"I'm selling the building," he said.

PROFESSIONAL. IN AND OUT. That had been Barrie's plan when Betty apologetically told her that Curtis was waiting in the barn with the sick calf. And seeing him again… He was older, obviously, but he was still the same Curtis who was too ruggedly handsome for his own good. But she was fifteen years older this time around, and pregnant. She had bigger worries than Curtis's ability to make her melt with one of his half smiles. Besides, there was a far higher risk of him irritating her. She didn't have the patience to deal with his boyish whims—her life had been turned upside down with this pregnancy, and she was facing her first Christmas without her mom, who had passed away last February from a stroke. She hadn't seen that heartbreak coming, either.

"Selling the building?" she repeated, slipping past him into the aisle, his words not sinking in.

"The commercial building my uncle left me—the one you lease for your practice."

Barrie whipped around in shock. "Wait—what?"

"I don't have much choice, Barrie."

"Selling it to who?" she demanded. A change in ownership didn't have to mean an end to her ability to lease there… Her mind spun forward, sifting through the possibilities.

"Nothing's finalized," he replied.

As if that made his intentions any different. Anger simmered beneath the surface. She'd worked too hard for this, for too long, but Curtis had never cared about her ambitions. Fifteen years hadn't changed much between them. What she needed was information—then she could make a plan. She'd had too many surprises lately, and a plan was an absolute necessity.

"But you have an interested buyer," she countered.

"Palmer Berton is interested, but we haven't nailed anything down."

Barrie swallowed hard, her stomach dropping.

"You're going to sell the building that houses my clinic to my business rival," she clarified. "And you think he'll keep leasing to me? I'm going to have to find a new place—move all my equipment, renovate the new space…" She was already tallying the cost of this, and as the tally rose, so did her anxiety. "Why are you doing this?"

"It's not personal," he said. "I need to liquidate."

Not personal? Curtis of all people knew how personal her practice was to her. "You need the money *now*?"

"I'm going to buy a stud farm with my business partner in Wyoming, and I need to sell to get the money for my half of the down payment. I don't have a choice, Barrie."

"So, what happened to bull riding?" She couldn't control the ice in her tone. That had been the cause of their divorce—bull riding had stayed his priority, leaving her in the dust. She'd wanted a real home with him, not to follow after him in a beat-up trailer. She'd wanted to start a family, to pursue her education and become a vet. She'd wanted a life, not a road trip.

"My body can't take it anymore," he replied. "I've broken too many bones. This wrist—" He held up his arm and moved his hand in a circle. "You hear that clicking? Both of my ankles do that, too. I've gone as far as I can in the circuit. I'm officially old."

At thirty-seven. Barrie had seen that coming, too, but he'd never listened to her. A body could take only so much punishment, and every time he'd get thrown and break a rib or dislocate his shoulder, she'd be the one patching up his injuries and begging him to find something safer, something more reliable… How many times had she sat in her parents' kitchen, describing some new injury to her mom, who wisely just listened and offered no advice?

"That's it, then," she said. "You're selling and this is my heads-up."

He didn't answer. She sighed and hitched her bag up on her shoulder.

"Fine," she said. "Thanks for the warning."

Since when had Curtis been stable, anyway? This had always been the problem—Curtis was always on the move. Leasing from his uncle had seemed safe enough, but when he died of a heart attack last year and left the building to Curtis, she'd had a sinking suspicion that her comfortably predictable days were limited. She paid her monthly lease to a management company, and she'd hoped that arrangement could continue for a while.

"You don't know that Palmer will kick you out," Curtis said.

"Really?" she snapped. "Because I know Palmer pretty well. I worked under him for three years after I got my doctorate degree. He was furious when I started my own practice. He hates competition. I'm still under water on my student loans, I owe a good amount for supplies and renovating my clinic… I've only been running my own practice for four years! If you need help with that math, I'm nowhere near financially stable enough to ride this out."

Plus, there was the baby, which complicated everything further. She'd been wondering how she'd run a veterinary practice with a newborn. If her mom were still with them, she'd have a solution, but Mom was gone, and Barrie would have to sort this out on her own. Vets were on call 24/7. That was the way things worked in this field, and she wouldn't be able to afford to take a decent maternity leave. She ran a hand over her belly and the baby squirmed in response. Emotion rose in her chest, and she swallowed against it.

"What am I supposed to do?" Curtis's tone softened. "I own the building, but I can't do a thing unless I sell it. I'm sorry, Barrie. I mean it when I say selling the building isn't personal. I've put off the sale for a year, and there isn't any other way. I can't do the circuit anymore, and I have a chance for a fresh start. I either sell and invest in a business, or I'm washed up. It's as simple as that."

"It's you or me," she said wryly. "Nothing's changed, has it?"

Curtis took off his cowboy hat and scrubbed a hand through his hair. "We always did want different things."

"Yeah." The baby poked out a foot—maybe a hand? She put her own hand over the spot. Would she be forced to give up her dream of running her own practice and work under Palmer Berton again? The very thought put a sour taste in her mouth.

"Barrie, I'm sorry."

"You keep saying that." She shot him a chilly smile. "But let's keep things professional. I'm here as your vet, not as your ex-wife. If you notice any more cattle with hanging heads, lethargy or nasal discharge, call me and we'll treat them right away. We can get this under control if we're careful."

Curtis blinked, then nodded. Had he expected her not to be professional? He'd been gone a long time, and life hadn't just stopped in his absence. He might have wasted his time on the circuit, but she'd made good use of hers. Ironically, he could still pulverize her plans—that had been Curtis's greatest talent.

"Okay," he said. "I'll keep an eye out and give you a call. Unless you'd rather we call Palmer so you don't have to deal with me."

And give Palmer the job? No, she didn't want that in the least. She still had a practice to run, and she'd need all the money she could squirrel away.

"Curtis, I'm a professional," she replied. "And I'm good at what I do. Call me."

He nodded. "Will do."

Curtis—or at least, her feelings for him—had been at the center of all of Barrie's biggest mistakes in life, starting with marrying him and ending with a very unplanned pregnancy. This baby wasn't his, obviously, but he'd been unwittingly connected.

As she headed back to her truck, Barrie let out a wavering sigh.

Professional. In and out. She'd managed it, hadn't she?

One thing was certain—she wasn't going to let Curtis close enough to mess with her heart again. He'd already done enough damage for a lifetime.

Chapter Two

That evening, Curtis sank into a kitchen chair while Aunt Betty dished up a big plate of shepherd's pie and placed it in front of him. She wore a walking cast—cumbersome and awkward, but she still got from place to place. Heaven help her if she tried to get onto a horse, though.

It was only dinnertime, but outside the kitchen window the sky was black. Curtis had more work to finish up before he was done for the day; this was just a food break. He'd forgotten how much work a ranch was. Bull riding came with training and practice, but running a ranch was the kind of work that never ended—there was no night off.

"Barrie says the virus is containable," Betty said, flipping her gray braid back over her shoulder. "That's a relief. I should have kept a closer eye on those calves myself."

"Now we know," Curtis replied. "I've got the other ranch hands keeping an eye out, too, so we should be able to keep it from spreading."

Betty dished herself up a plate of shepherd's pie, as

well, then deposited it on the table with a clunk. His aunt's shepherd's pie was amazing—spicy meat, creamy potatoes and a perfectly cooked layer of green peas.

"You didn't tell me Barrie was pregnant," Curtis added. He'd been thinking about Barrie all day after seeing her in the barn. He'd known he'd run into her eventually, but he'd halfway hoped he'd have some control over that. Might have made it easier, too, if his aunt had given him more than a minute's warning.

Betty pulled her chair out with a scrape and sat down. "Any chance the baby is yours?"

Curtis shot her an incredulous look. "Of course not."

"Then it was hardly your concern," Betty retorted.

That sounded real familiar, and he shot his aunt a wry smile. "Fine. Point made."

They both started to eat, and for a few moments, Curtis thought the conversation might be over, but then his aunt said, "This town has been gossiping something fierce, and I wasn't about to be part of that. Everyone has a theory on who the father is, and Barrie isn't saying."

"I noticed that. I asked her about it, and she pretty much told me to mind my own business." He reached for the pitcher of milk and poured them each a glass.

Betty's expression softened. "She's not yours to worry over anymore, Curtis."

"I know that." He took another bite and glanced out the window again. Snow swirled against the glass.

"Do you?" Betty asked.

He sighed. "I'm not here for Barrie, Aunty. I'm here

to take care of my business, help you out and be on my way."

Betty didn't answer, but she got that look on her face that said she thought she knew better.

"I told her that I'm selling the building," he added.

"And how did that go down?" Betty asked.

"Not well, I have to admit." Curtis sighed. "She says that Palmer will push her out of business."

"And he will."

Curtis put down his fork. What made everyone so certain? "Palmer isn't the devil. Maybe he just wants a real estate investment. That isn't unheard of."

Betty shrugged. "She's a better vet."

"Is she?" Curtis had never seen Barrie in her professional capacity until today, and while he'd been impressed by her competence, he couldn't judge much. Back when they'd been married, she'd wanted to go to school, but that hadn't happened yet. Her life—everything she'd built for herself—had come together after he'd left town. It was slightly intimidating. She'd become a talented vet, and he'd become…too old to bull ride.

"Palmer has more experience, obviously," Betty said, "but she's got better instincts. Working together, they were a great team. On her own, Barrie has more potential. Palmer has already peaked in his career. She's still climbing."

"So you think he's threatened," Curtis concluded.

"If he's smart, he is."

An unbidden wave of pride rose up inside him. Barrie had always wanted to be a vet, and she'd not only achieved her dream, she was better than the established vet here in town, too. He'd always felt proud of Barrie when they were together. She was smarter than he was, in the book sense, at least. That had been frustrating when they'd argued, though. When she got mad, she got articulate. When he got mad, it all just balled up and he went out to ride until it untangled. Even their fighting hadn't been compatible.

"So she's doing well, then," he said.

"Besides her mother passing away last winter," his aunt said. "I told you about the funeral, right?"

"Yeah." He sobered. Gwyneth Jones had never been his biggest fan, but she'd been a good woman, and he'd been sad to hear about her passing. This was a hard year for Barrie, and he hated to contribute to her difficulties, but he didn't have a whole lot of choice.

"She's done really well in her practice," Betty went on. "She's still single, though."

"So are you," he quipped. "We aren't still judging people's worth by their marital status, are we?"

"Of course not," Betty said. "It's not like I'm one to talk. But I'm more of the saintly single type," she replied with a small smile. "It suits me."

Curtis chuckled. "And Barrie isn't?"

"She's more like you," Betty said, reaching past Curtis for a dinner roll. "Damaged."

"Ouch." Was that really how Betty saw him?

"You don't count on me for flattery," she replied, taking a bite. "You count on me for honesty."

"Fine." That was true. Betty had always been a rock in that sense. "So, we both know why I'm a wreck. Why is she?"

"In my humble opinion? It's because of you."

Curtis's humor evaporated as his aunt's words landed. "What do you mean?"

"She never did bounce back, dear."

Barrie had always been tough, beautiful and definitely desired by the other guys in town. He'd tormented himself for years thinking about the cowboys who would have gladly moved in to fill the void he left behind. Over the last decade, he hadn't called his aunt terribly often. When he did, and when he'd asked about Barrie, there was normally a boyfriend in the mix somewhere.

"I know she dated," he countered. "You told me that much."

"Oh, she dated," Betty said with a nod. "She's always been a beautiful girl. But she never did get anywhere near marriage again."

Neither had he, for that matter. As a bull rider, women had come to him, and he hadn't had to put a whole lot of effort into it. But he hadn't gotten serious. He told himself it was because he'd been married before, and he wasn't the romantic type anymore. Marriage was a whole lot harder than he'd anticipated. He'd done everything he could think of to make Barrie happy, and he still hadn't been enough for her. He wasn't a glutton for punishment, but he'd never imagined that she had ended up just as jaded as he had.

"I have to tell you, Curtis," his aunt went on, "the gossip has been vicious about Barrie."

"She isn't the first person to have a child outside wedlock in this town," he pointed out.

"No, she isn't," Betty confirmed. "But she won't say who the father is, and people's imaginations can come up with a whole lot more scandal than is probably the case."

"Like what?" he asked.

"Some suggest she's had an affair with a married guy around town. I know one woman who has an itemized list on why she's confident that the mayor is the father. Others say she's given up on finding love and went to a sperm clinic—" Betty paused. "Does it even matter? My point is that this isn't an easy time for Barrie. And maybe you could…consider all of that."

"When selling the building, you mean," he clarified.

"Yes."

"Aunty," he said slowly. "If I'm going to buy that stud farm, then I'm on a timeline. I need to liquidate and come up with my half of the down payment by Christmas Eve, or the deal is off. I feel for Barrie— losing her mom, all of it—but we've been researching this business venture for two years now, and this sale is not only an excellent price, but it would be a future away from bull riding. This is no whim—it's a plan."

"I know that," his aunt replied.

"So you can see that I don't have a lot of options here," he said. "Barrie has her practice. She's built a life for herself. It's been tough—I can see that—but she's got a life put together. I have to do the same thing."

Betty sighed. "I know. I just… Be as kind as possible, okay?"

"I'll do my best."

But what his aunt expected of him, he had no idea.

None of this was his fault. If he didn't invest in something soon, he wouldn't be able to provide for anyone, let alone himself. If he didn't sort out his own life, no one else was going to do it for him.

Except providing for someone else hadn't even entered his mind until this moment...and along with the thought was an image of pregnant Barrie. He pushed it back—Barrie wasn't his to worry about anymore. Besides, while she'd lost her mom, she had the whole town of Hope to back her up. The locals might enjoy some salacious gossip, but when it came right down to it, they took care of their own. He ate his last bite and rose to his feet.

"I've got more cattle to check on," he said. "Thanks for dinner. Delicious as always."

"Thanks for helping out," Betty replied. "I mean that, Curtis. From the bottom of my heart."

Curtis wiped his mouth with a napkin and deposited the plate in the kitchen sink. Shooting his aunt a grin, he headed for the door.

Barrie was independent. She'd fought him every day of their marriage and then proceeded to get her education and build a veterinary practice on her own. She was a force to be reckoned with, and while he understood his aunt's concern about Barrie right now, he'd be smart to follow his carefully laid plans and start a life away from the circuit. That's what Barrie had always wanted him to do, wasn't it? And she'd been right. Better late than never.

He stepped into his boots and looked out at the ranch truck, snow accumulating over the hood in a smooth sheet. Snow was floating down in big fluffy flakes, and his mind was skipping ahead to the cattle. Curtis pushed his hat onto his head and trudged out into the cold.

Short days and long nights. This time of year brought the solstice, the shortest, coldest days before daylight started pushing back once more...

He glanced over his shoulder at the cheery glow of indoor lights shining through the windows. He was back in Hope for Christmas, and it wasn't going to be a cheery homecoming. But he'd get through it and hold out for spring and new beginnings.

THE NEXT MORNING, Barrie awoke three minutes before her alarm went off...and her feet were already sore. Her Great Dane, Miley, stood at her bedside, soulful eyes fixed on her. She'd never had trouble with her feet before, but pregnancy seemed to be changing the rules on her, and she hated that. When she'd first found out that she was pregnant, she'd promised herself nothing needed to change until the baby actually arrived. Some women nested when they were pregnant, but Barrie was going to control that instinct. These last few months would allow her to build up her practice enough that after the baby came she could scale back to clinic hours only, cut out the after-hours emergency calls and still keep her business afloat. But her body seemed to have other ideas.

"Morning, Miley," she said, reaching from under her cozy comforter to give the massive dog an affectionate ear scratch. He'd started out as a regular-sized puppy with paws like dinner plates, and he'd grown past even ordinary Great Dane proportions. He was a huge, jowly, slate-gray lap dog—at least, that's how he saw himself. He was a big baby, and absolutely worthless as a guard dog, but she loved him.

Barrie rolled out of bed and ran her hand over her belly. The baby stretched inside her. She didn't know if she was having a boy or a girl yet. She'd tried to find out at her last ultrasound, but the baby's legs were firmly crossed. She'd try to find out again—planning was key, and she didn't have the luxury of sweet surprises.

She pulled her bathrobe around her body and cinched it above her belly. She was ever growing, and as she passed her full-length mirror before she padded out into the hallway, she caught a glimpse of a rounded, bed-headed stranger with a colt-sized dog trailing after her. There was no getting used to this, but she did enjoy it. She'd always wanted kids—the nonfurry kind—and while the timing wasn't great, she was finally going to be a mother. It wasn't quite how she'd imagined it happening… At least she'd get a chance at motherhood, and still being single at the age of thirty-seven, she'd started to give up hope.

Barrie lived in a single-level ranch house on the north end of Hope. She looked out her kitchen window at the pristine snow from last night's storm. The neighbor kid she paid to shovel her driveway was already at it, metal scraping against asphalt. This morning, she had plans to organize her presentation for Hope's 4-H club. She'd been invited to speak about a woman's contribution to agriculture, and that was a subject Barrie was passionate about. Girls needed encouragement to step out and become leaders in ranching and animal care. If there was one thing Barrie knew, it was that a woman couldn't wait for a man to define her future.

"You hungry, Miley?" She pulled down his food dish—which was really a medium-sized mixing bowl—took out the bag of dog food and filled the bowl to the top. Miley hopped up, paws on the counter, and snuffled his nose toward the bag.

"Miley!" she said reproachfully, and he dropped back down to the floor. He didn't need his paws on the counter to see over it. When she put his bowl on the floor, he immediately dropped his face into it and started to gobble.

While Miley ate, she headed to the fridge to find her own breakfast. She felt just about as hungry as the dog. She grabbed a bag of bagels from the fridge and a tub of cream cheese. Then her cell phone rang, and she picked it up from the counter and punched the speaker button.

"Dr. Jones, veterinary medicine," she said.

"Barrie?" She knew his voice right away, and she froze in the middle of cutting a bagel. Why did he have to sound like the same old Curtis? Her heart clenched, and she had to remind herself to exhale. Miley looked over at her, sensing her tension, no doubt.

"Curtis," she said, resuming what she was doing and attempting to keep her voice casual. "Everything okay over there?"

"We have another sick cow."

Bovine respiratory disease could spread quickly in the right conditions, and it could decimate a herd if left unchecked.

"A calf?" she asked.

"No, this is a full-grown heifer," he replied. "It's out in the south field. I saw it this morning on my rounds, and she's too big to just tip into the bed of a pickup and bring back to the barn, so I was wondering what the best course of action is in this kind of situation."

Barrie sank a butter knife into the cream cheese and began spreading it onto her bagel. This was going to be a breakfast to go.

"I'll leave in about ten minutes," she said. "I'll go with you to see her in the field. We might be able to leave her where she is, depending on how sick she is."

"Great." He paused. "You sure this is okay? Not too early?"

Barrie rolled her eyes. She was pregnant, not an invalid. She hated the kid gloves men used with her now that she was expecting, but there didn't seem to be any avoiding it. Perhaps this could turn into a nice little anecdote for her presentation to the 4-H girls.

"I'm a vet, Curtis," she said wryly. "This is the job."

"Of course." His tone softened. "See you soon."

Barrie hung up the phone and took a jaw-cracking bite of her bagel. "Eat up, Miley," she said past a mouthful of food. "We're leaving."

Ten minutes later, Barrie was dressed, Miley had finished his breakfast and she had her own breakfast in a plastic container on the seat beside her. Her veterinary bag and other portable equipment were in the bed of the truck, and Miley was in the back seat, breathing dog breath over her shoulder. He was the worst back seat driver.

"Miley, give me some space," she said, pushing his jowly face away from hers. "Miley!"

He ignored her until she pointed and said, "Lie down, Miley."

Miley heaved a sigh and folded himself into the seat, his nails scratching against the vinyl. Lying down back there was no easy feat for a dog Miley's size.

"Good dog," she said with a smile. "You're my boy, aren't you?"

Miley made a conversational growling noise. It was his way of giving a verbal reply without getting into trouble for barking in the vehicle, and Barrie put her attention into driving.

Betty Porter's ranch was about forty minutes outside Hope. Barrie had done some work with Betty's livestock in the past few years, but her most vivid memories of the place would always be from when she'd been married to Curtis. They used to go to Betty's place for dinner sometimes, and it had always been so warm and cozy. Curtis used to slide a hand up her leg under the table, which had embarrassed Barrie to no end. It amused Curtis just as much when she'd blush and Betty would give her a quizzical look. Barrie pushed the memories away.

She'd been in love with the soft-hearted rebel in Curtis, but that rebellious streak also made living with him difficult. Curtis was better at sneaking out to see her than he was at coming home to see her. He'd been better at seducing than he was at supporting.

And he was back. Seeing him again stirred up a confusing cocktail of old feelings. She'd married a bull rider but hadn't been successful in taming him. That was how wisdom was earned—through mistakes—but even if she hadn't married him, she'd have lived to regret it. Curtis Porter was a no-win situation.

The miles and minutes clicked past as she ate her breakfast one-handed, and before too long, she came up on the side road that led to the Porter ranch. She signaled and turned, scanning the familiar landscape. This mile marker, the copse of trees at the edge of the first field…she knew this area like the back of her hand.

Dealing with her memories of Curtis was hard enough, but adding the real man into the mix seemed foolhardy, even now. Why couldn't he have just stayed away? The timing was awful—she was already off balance with the baby coming and her mom's recent death. If it weren't for her pregnancy, she might have been able to deal with all of this more easily…maybe.

Miley started scrambling again as he tried to get up.

"Hold on, Miley," she said as she turned in to the gravel drive. "Almost there."

Barrie took Miley with her on veterinary calls quite often. Not only was he good company, but she felt safer with him at her side, too. Not every ranch was equally well run, and some of them housed some rather slimy employees who stepped just a little more carefully around her with a dog Miley's size staring them down. He'd never been tested to see how far he'd go to protect his mistress, and that was probably for the best.

Barrie pulled to a stop next to the ranch house and turned off the engine. The front door opened almost immediately and Curtis came outside. He was already in a coat and boots. He'd always been a tall man, but he looked broader and bulkier now that he was firmly in his manhood. If only he'd aged a little less attractively…

"Alright, Miley," she said quietly. "Let's go."

Barrie pushed open her door and hopped out, then opened the back door for Miley, who followed her. Curtis's step hitched just once as his gaze landed on the dog, and she couldn't help the smile that twitched at her lips at his reaction.

"You rode bulls," she said wryly. "This big old baby shouldn't be a problem."

"He's almost as tall, too…" Curtis put out a tentative hand, and Miley sniffed him.

"Meet Miley," she said. "He's my right-hand dog."

"Hey…" Curtis let Miley sniff him again, then stroked the top of Miley's gray head. "You're a big fella."

Miley rolled his eyes back in ecstasy and nuzzled closer to Curtis like the big baby he was. She heaved a sigh. When Miley looked back at her, the dog froze for a moment, his eyes locked on his mistress.

"You're a traitor," she said with a low laugh.

Miley, reassured that there was no actual danger, turned his attention to sniffing the ground and finding a place to pee.

"So, are you ready to head out to the field?" Curtis asked.

"Absolutely. Let me get my bag." Barrie went around her truck and opened the back to get her supplies. Then she met him at the ranch truck they'd take out into the field.

"Is…*he* coming?" Curtis asked dubiously.

Betty opened the side door at that moment, and when she spotted Miley, her face crinkled into a smile.

"Oh, you handsome young man!" she exclaimed. "Come over here, Miley. Betty has some treats for her boy!"

Curtis shot his aunt a look of surprise and Barrie chuckled. "They're already acquainted."

"Looks like," Curtis replied with a shake of his head.

Betty disappeared into the house, Miley joyfully bounding behind her. The screen door slammed shut, and Curtis faced her with one side of his mouth turned up in a smile.

"Lead the way," she said, jutting her chin toward the rusty red Chevy. She wouldn't be softened by him. At this point, she was immune to his charms. Besides, Curtis Porter was selling her out. He might not owe her a blasted thing anymore, especially when it came to that particular piece of property, but he still had the uncanny ability to turn her entire life upside down just by waltzing into town. And she hated that. His fingerprints were still on her life, and she couldn't ever quite scrub them off.

So Curtis was back, and he was screwing her over, but in the meantime, he was a paying customer and Barrie couldn't afford to be choosy.

Chapter Three

Curtis opened the passenger side door and held out his hand. Barrie stepped smoothly past him and awkwardly hoisted herself up into the seat without his aid. He shook his head. Just like old times.

"It's a hand up," he said with a wry smile, "nothing more."

And he meant that. He wasn't foolish enough to try something with her again. He already knew how that ended, and he was no longer a twenty-year-old pup looking to belong somewhere. The last fifteen years had solidified him, too. He'd learned about himself—his strengths and weaknesses, as well as what he wanted out of life: a job he could rely on, a place where he could make a difference and earn some respect. Just once, he wanted to be called Mister.

"I'm fine." Barrie met his gaze with a cool smile of her own, and he adjusted his hat, then handed her the leather veterinary bag. She'd never really needed him for anything, and that had chafed.

Curtis slammed the door shut and headed around to the driver's side. The south field was a fifteen-minute drive. Earlier he'd brought the cow some hay and a bucket of water and tossed a saddle blanket over its back to keep it warm until he could bring Barrie out there. He started the truck and cranked up the heat.

"That's some dog you've got there," he said as he turned onto the gravel road that led past the barn and down toward the pasture.

"Miley's my baby," she said, and he noticed her rub a hand over her belly out of the corner of his eye. He was still getting used to this—the pregnant Barrie. She looked softer this way, more vulnerable, but looks were obviously deceiving, at least as far as her feelings for him were concerned.

"Until you have this one, at least," he said, nodding toward her belly.

"Miley will still be my baby," she replied, then sighed. "But yes, it'll be different. I honestly didn't think I'd end up having kids, so I may have set Miley up with some grand expectations."

"You always wanted kids, though," he countered.

"I know, but sometimes life works out different than you planned," she replied. "Exhibit number one, right here." She patted her belly.

According to Aunt Betty, he'd been the reason she stayed single and childless, and he didn't like that theory. So their marriage hadn't lasted. The rest of her life's choices couldn't be blamed on him any more than her successes could be attributed to him. He stayed silent for a few beats.

"What?" she said.

"Betty kind of—" How much of this should he even tell her? "She said I'd done a real number on you."

"You did," she retorted. "But like I said, I'm fine."

"So you don't blame me for…anything?"

"Oh, I hold a grudge, Curtis." She shot him a rueful smile. "But you'll just have to live with that. Divorces come with grudges built in."

Curtis nodded. "Alright. I guess I can accept that."

Besides, from where he was sitting, her life hadn't turned out so bad. And as for the kids—she was having a baby, wasn't she?

"So, you're done with bull riding, then?" she asked.

"Yeah." She'd been right about the longevity of it. "It's tough on a body. I can't keep it up. Besides, it's time to do something where I can grow old."

"Like a stud farm," she said.

"Yep. As half owner, I'll be managing the place, not doing the physical labor."

She nodded. "It's smart. I'll give you that."

"Thanks."

"Will you miss it—the bull riding, I mean?"

He rubbed his hand down his thigh toward his knee, which had started to ache with the cold. There was something about those eight seconds in the ring that grew him in ways Barrie had never understood. It was man against beast, skill against fury. He was proving himself in there—time after time—learning from mistakes and fine-tuning his game. He never felt more alive than when he was on the back of an enraged bull.

"Yeah," he admitted. "I will miss it. I do already. My heart hasn't caught up with my age yet, I guess."

"It never did." Her tone was dry, and she cast him one unreadable look.

He chuckled. "Is that the grudge?"

"Yep." And there wasn't even a glimmer of humor in her eye.

But that wasn't entirely fair, either. They'd been opposites, which was part of the fuel of their passion. She was almost regal, and he was the scruffy cowboy. She came from a good family, and he came from a chronically overworked single mom who'd consistently chosen boyfriends over him. Barrie had been the unblemished one, the one life hadn't knocked around yet, and he'd already been through more than she could fully comprehend by the time he'd landed in Hope at the ripe old age of sixteen. If anyone should have been the obsessive planner at that point, most people would have assumed it was Curtis—just needing a bit of stability—but it had been Barrie who wanted everything nailed down and safe. And she had her untainted life here in Hope as her proof that her way was better than his. What did a scuffed-up cowboy like him know about a calm and secure life?

Curtis had known exactly how lucky he was to have her in his life, and his heart had been in their marriage. The problem, as he saw it, was that she hadn't trusted him enough to risk a single thing after those vows. He'd wanted to make something of himself, and she'd dug in her heels and refused to budge. Her safe and secure life was here in Hope, and he was welcome to stay there with her, but she hadn't trusted him beyond those town limits. So he had a grudge or two of his own.

"How is your dad?" he asked, changing the subject.

"As well as can be expected since Mom passed away. He's looking at retirement in the next couple of years."

"He isn't retired yet?" Curtis asked. "He's got to be, what, seventy?"

"Sixty-nine," she replied. "And who can afford to retire these days?"

Sixty-nine and still working as a cattle mover—that would take a toll on a body, too, but Steve Jones didn't have the luxury of a career change.

"I'm sorry about your mom," he added. "Betty told me about her passing away when it happened, but I didn't think you'd want to hear from me."

"Thanks." She didn't clarify if he'd made the right call in staying clear, so he'd just assume he'd been right. He was the ex-husband, after all. Not exactly a comfort.

"That must have been a shock," he said.

"Yeah." She sighed. "You don't see that coming. This will be our first Christmas without her."

"I'm sorry, Barrie."

"Me, too." She was silent for a moment. "I guess you'll have Christmas with Betty, then."

"I need to have the sale finalized by Christmas Eve," he said. "Betty says she could do without me by then, so, yeah. Christmas with Betty, and then I'm leaving."

"So I'll be screwed over by Christmas." Her tone was low and quiet, but he heard the barb in her words.

"Barrie, this isn't personal!" He shook his head. "You, of all people, should appreciate my situation. Your dad is in the same boat—working a physical job that takes a toll on a body—"

"Leave my father out of this."

Curtis had crossed a line; her dad's plans were none of his business, and he knew that. It was hard to come back to Hope and pretend that the people he'd known so well were strangers again just because he and Barrie had broken up. Mr. and Mrs. Jones had been a huge part of his life back then, but obviously, her father would feel different about him postdivorce.

"Like I said before, you were right," he said. "Bull riding was hard on my body, and this isn't a matter of choice anymore. I simply can't keep going. My joints are shot, I've broken more bones than I can count, and I couldn't get on another bull if I wanted to. You told me all those years ago that this would happen, and I said I was tough enough to handle it. And I was—until now. So... I don't have a lot of choice here, Barrie. I have to establish a new career and get some money in the bank so I can retire at a reasonable time."

She sighed and adjusted the bag on her lap. "I always thought saying I told you so would feel better than this."

Curtis smiled ruefully. Yeah, well, he'd always thought hearing it would sting more. But fifteen years had a way of evening the scales, it seemed. She used to be the one with all the cards, and now he was getting his turn at being the one with the leverage. Still, tilling her under hadn't been the plan...

"You worked with Palmer before," Curtis said. "Would it be so terrible if you ended up working together again? You've got some loyal clients—"

"I worked too hard to get my own practice to just

cave in like that," she interrupted. "And no offense, Curtis, but I don't need you to solve this for me."

"Just trying to help," he said. Which really felt like the least he could do considering that he was selling the building to her direct rival.

"Well, don't. I'll figure it out."

The same old Barrie—single-minded, stubborn as all get-out and perfectly capable of sorting out her own life. That's what their married life had been—her way. And if you just looked at what she'd done with herself in the last fifteen years, it could be argued that the best thing he'd ever done for her was to get out of her way. He'd never been a part of her success—and she hadn't been a part of his. From this side of things, it looked like a life with him had only slowed her down.

The truck rumbled over the snowy road, tires following the tracks from that morning. Fresh snow drifted against the fence posts and capped them with leaning towers of snow. Beyond the barbed wire, the snow-laden hills rolled out toward the mountains, the peaks disappearing into cloud cover. He'd learned to love this land those few years he'd stayed with his aunt, and having Barrie by his side as he drove out this way was frustrating. Curtis might be a constant irritation to Barrie—even now, he was realizing—but he wasn't useless, either. So if he and Barrie were only going to butt heads, he might as well focus on the work ahead of them.

"We're almost there," he said. "Around this next corner."

Barrie sat up a little straighter, her attention out the window.

"I left the cow with some feed and a blanket—you know, just in case. I wasn't sure how sick it was, so—"

"That was a good call," she said, glancing around. "How far out into the field is it?"

"A few yards," he said. "Not too far. I found it when I was filling feeders this morning."

He pulled up to the gate that allowed trucks access to feeders in the field, and got out to open it. The cows looked up at him in mild curiosity—an older calf ambling over as if interested in some freedom beyond the fence.

"Hya!" he said, and the calf veered off. Curtis jumped back into the cab and drove into the pasture, then hopped out again to close the gate behind them. By the time the gate was locked and he'd come back to the truck, Barrie was standing in the snow, her bag held in front of her belly almost protectively. Her hair ruffled around her face in the icy wind, and her breath clouded as she scanned the cattle that were present, her practiced gaze moving over them slowly. She was irritatingly beautiful—that was the first thing he remembered thinking when he'd met her in senior year. She was the kind of gorgeous that didn't need what he had to offer, but he couldn't help offering it anyway.

"The cow's over—" he began, but Barrie was already walking in the direction of the cow about twenty yards away now. The cow had shaken off the blanket, and the rumpled material lay in the snow another few yards off.

"I see her," Barrie said over her shoulder.

Once—just once—couldn't Barrie be a step behind him? But whatever. They were here for a cow, and not their complex history. If she wanted to know why he needed a new start so badly, here was a prime example.

"Lead the way," he muttered. It's what she'd always done, anyway.

THE COW WAS definitely ill; she could tell by the way the animal stood. As she got closer, she could make out nasal discharge, the bovine equivalent of a runny nose. The snow was deep, and she had to raise her feet high to get through it, something that was harder now that she was pregnant. Her breath was coming in gasps by the time she approached the cow. She had to pause to catch her breath, and she glanced back to see Curtis's tall form close behind.

It felt odd to have Curtis in town, and something had been nagging at her since she'd seen him in the barn last night—how come this was the first she'd seen of him in fifteen years? Betty was in Hope, and she'd been like a second mother to him. He'd walked out of town and come back only once—to finalize their divorce. Did he hate Barrie that much by the end of their marriage?

She looked around the snowy field, gauging the cow's flight path. When handling cattle, it was important to make sure they had a free escape route, or the cow might panic, and two thousand pounds of scared bovine could be incredibly dangerous. She couldn't allow herself to be distracted.

"You never visited Hope," she said as he stopped at her side.

"Sure I did."

She looked over in surprise. "When? I never saw you."

"A few Christmases. I didn't call friends or anything. I just had a day or two with Betty and headed on out again."

"I didn't realize that." She licked her lips. "Why the secrecy?"

"It wasn't a secret visit, just streamlined. I didn't really keep up with people from high school. I came to see Betty."

She eyed him speculatively. "You weren't avoiding me, were you?"

His lips turned up into a wry smile. "Why would I avoid you?"

Barrie sighed and turned back to the cow. She felt the cow's belly. It hadn't been eating much—like the calf—but the belly wasn't completely empty, either. The cow shifted its weight from side to side, and she took a step back.

"Maybe the same reason you left in the first place," she replied, her voice low.

"You really wanted me dropping in on your family Christmases?" he asked.

"No." She sighed. She wasn't sure what she wanted—absolution, maybe. She hadn't been the wife she'd tried to be back then, but now, as a mature woman, she wasn't sure that her image of perfection had been realistic. It certainly hadn't included the fights they used to have…

Barrie liked the challenge of taming a wild spirit when it came to horses and cattle, but she resented that same wild spirit when it came to her husband. Marriage meant hearth and home to her, but to Curtis, it had been a beat-up trailer parked wherever he was bull riding.

But he'd come back for Christmas with Betty a few times, and somehow that stung.

"I meant well, you know," she added. "I only ever tried to make a home for you."

"I was a bull rider," he replied. "You knew all of that before you married me."

"Most men settle down when they get married," she countered. "A wife should change something."

"Not my identity. You wanted me to act like a different man."

"I wanted you to act like a *married* man!"

The old irritation flooded back, and she hated that. She'd come a long way in the last fifteen years, and it felt petty to slide back into those old arguments. She wasn't the same person anymore, either.

"I never cheated on you," Curtis countered.

"There is more to marriage than monogamy," she said. "You had a *home* with me, Curtis. You treated it more like a hotel room."

"In all the best ways." He shot her a teasing look, and she rolled her eyes in response. They might have shared a passionate relationship, but that hadn't been enough. She'd been the fool who'd married a man based on love and her belief in his potential.

"Forget it," she said with a sigh. "It was a long time ago. I'm sorry to have brought it up." This was exactly why they hadn't worked out. They talked at cross purposes, but maybe he was right—she'd been trying to change him. She was wise enough now not to try that again.

Barrie turned her attention back to the cow. She checked its temperature, and while she couldn't tell exactly how sick the animal was by temperature alone, it had a low fever. All the signs were here—the illness was spreading, apparently. She patted the cow's rump, and it didn't move.

"We wanted different things, Barrie," he said. "You wanted that white picket fence that would please your parents and give you some respect around here. I didn't care about Hope's respect. I wanted some adventure. We just…clashed, I guess."

Barrie dropped the thermometer back into her bag, and pulled out a fresh syringe and the bottle of medication. Yes, she'd wanted a respectable home, and she'd worked hard to create it. A garden in the backyard, flowers in the front… He'd never cared to put down his roots where she'd turned up the soil.

"Quite simple, really," she said with a sigh. "And we'd been young enough to think it wouldn't matter." She turned back toward the cow. "I'll give the antibiotic shot. It'll boost her recovery."

"You're the expert," he replied, and she glanced back to see Curtis standing there with his hands shoved into his jacket pockets. The wind had reddened his cheeks, and she had to admit that he had aged. In a good way, though. He wasn't like some of those boys from high school who were bald under their baseball caps and sported beer bellies now that they were creeping up to forty. Curtis was in good shape.

Barrie prepared the syringe, then felt for the muscle along the flank. Her feet were cold in her boots, and the wind stung her fingers. Just as the needle hit flesh, the cow suddenly lunged, knocking Barrie off balance as it heaved forward.

The cow stepped back so fluidly that she wasn't able to pull herself out of the way quickly enough. But just before she was trampled, strong hands grabbed her by the coat and hauled her backward so fast that her breath stuck in her throat.

Barrie scrambled to get her feet underneath her, and Curtis lifted her almost effortlessly, then pulled her against him as she regained her balance. She was trapped in his strong arms, staring up into a face that was both achingly familiar and different at the same time.

"You've aged," she said feebly.

"Yeah?" He chuckled. "Is that how you thank a cowboy?"

"Thanks…" Her stomach did a flip as she straightened and pulled out of his arms. "I'll be fine."

Curtis cast her a dry look.

"What?" She smoothed her hand over her belly.

"How many times have you told me now that you're fine? I'm calling BS on that, Barrie. You aren't the least bit fine right now."

"The cow missed me—"

"That's not what I'm taking about, and you know it."

Barrie bent down to collect the syringe that had fallen into the snow. The cow had wandered off a couple of yards—maybe this particular cow had a bad experience with an immunization or something. Whatever had happened was all perfectly within the realms of normal when it came to a vet's daily duties. Granted, if she weren't pregnant, her reflexes might have been a bit faster...

"Curtis, you don't actually know me anymore."

"Hey," he said, his voice lowering. "You might not have liked the kind of husband I was, but I *was* your husband. I knew you, and I can recognize when you're freaked out."

Curtis might know some of her deeper characteristics, but that didn't mean he still knew how she thought and what could get a rise out of her. He'd missed fifteen years of personal growth. Besides, she hadn't been enough for him, so he could take his insights into her reactions and shove them.

"I'm not freaked out." She shot him an irritated look. "I'm *fine*."

She looked toward the cow again and adjusted the syringe, getting it ready for one more try.

"I don't need rescuing." Her fingers moved as she spoke. "So do what you have to do with that building, and I'll sort things out. I always have."

"Fair enough."

Barrie didn't want him to sell that building, but he'd already made it clear that he was out of options. If their divorce had taught her one thing, it was that she was better off facing facts and dealing with them. Hoping and wishing didn't help. She'd focus on her future with her child.

"And you'll need to quarantine that cow," she added.

"Yeah, I know. I'm not new to this, Barrie." His smile was slightly smug, but arguing with Curtis Porter about just about anything wasn't a great use of her time. *Professional. In and out.* What had happened to that excellent plan?

She headed toward the cow that had wandered off. She might be pregnant, and her life might be spinning right out of control at the moment, but she'd get through this by standing on her own two feet. Curtis was a cautionary tale—that was all.

Barrie took a deep breath, and let her tension go. The cattle could feel it. She patted the cow's rump, then inserted the needle into the tough flesh. She slowly depressed the plunger, then pulled the needle out and firmly rubbed the injection site.

"Done." She turned around and gave Curtis an arch look. "Like I said, quarantine that cow, and any others that appear sick. That's the fastest way to curb an outbreak."

Curtis might know her weaknesses, but she also knew his, and he was the furthest thing from reliable. She needed a plan and blinders, because with a baby on the way, she didn't have the luxury of being knocked off balance a second time by the same cowboy.

Chapter Four

The next morning, Barrie ran her hand over a golden Lab's silky head. This was Cody, the beloved pet of the Hartfield family, and he'd broken his leg while running on the ice. He was still unconscious from the sedative she'd given him, but his leg was set, the cast was in place and he'd recover just fine. His mistress, thirteen-year-old Melissa Hartfield, stood anxiously to the side. She wore her winter coat, open in the front, and a pair of puffy boots. She was a town kid—her dad was the mayor.

"Will he be okay?" Melissa asked. She looked younger than her age—her hair pulled back in a ponytail and her large eyes scanning the equipment. She glanced up at the IV inserted into a vein in the dog's leg, then down at the catheter Barrie had introduced to keep the dog comfortable while she worked. The catheter was out now.

"He'll be fine," Barrie reassured her. "It's not a bad break. I've put a cast on, and he'll have to wear a cone so he leaves the cast alone, poor boy. The cone is the worst part for them—it hits them in their dignity."

Melissa smiled faintly. "Will he be in pain?"

"I'll give you pain medication and some antibiotics. He'll need to take both daily—they're very important to help him rest more easily and to keep infection at bay."

"The IV—" Melissa looked intrigued. "How did you find his vein through his fur?"

"By touch." Barrie caught the girl's eye. "You're interested in veterinary medicine?"

Melissa's cheeks colored a little. "I want to be a vet like you when I grow up."

Barrie grinned. She never tired of talking to young people who wanted to follow in her footsteps. "That's great. And you can be. Just make sure you stay focused on school, because it's a long haul. And you can't let yourself get sidetracked by boys, either."

"That's what Mom always says," Melissa said with a roll of her eyes.

"Your mom is right," Barrie replied.

The front door to Barrie's clinic opened—she could hear the soft chime—and Melissa looked toward the door. Her mother, Jennifer Hartfield, would be arriving anytime now to pick them both up, but Barrie couldn't see the waiting room from where she stood.

"Is that your mom?" Barrie asked.

Melissa nodded.

"Let's bring Cody out to the waiting room, then," Barrie said. "You can take him home before he wakes up all the way. He'll be groggy for a few hours, but when he does wake up, you need to make sure he stays off this leg, okay?"

Melissa nodded. "Dr. Jones?"

"Hmm?" Barrie removed the IV and pressed some gauze over the puncture.

"I was wondering if you might need some help. I'm not asking for a job—I know I'm not old enough for that. But I could help out, and I'd really like to learn..."

Barrie shot the girl a smile. "I'll give that some thought, Melissa. I might be able to find something for you to do. And you'd have to get your mom's permission, of course. I'm going to be talking to the 4-H girls next week, so I'll see you then, too."

"Are you really?" Melissa asked. "That'll be cool."

"I'm looking forward to it."

Barrie set aside the last of the equipment and they wheeled the dog into the waiting room. Barrie was surprised to see both Jennifer Hartfield and Curtis standing by the line of chairs. He stood there like a tank—hat off but legs akimbo as he looked around. That dark gaze still gave her pause, even after all these years, and she shoved back those familiar feelings. Attraction had never been their problem. She gave Curtis a nod.

"Is there a problem with Betty's herd?" Barrie asked.

"Nope. Just came by." That dark gaze warmed, and she swallowed. Why did he have to do that? They weren't married anymore, and he had no right to go toying with her emotions when she was trying to work. She turned a smile to Jennifer.

"Cody is going to be fine," Barrie said, and she began explaining the care he'd need at home while his leg recovered. Jennifer and Melissa listened as she finished her explanation, and after Jennifer had paid the bill, they prepared to transfer Cody to the back of their SUV.

"Mom, Dr. Jones says that I might be able to help her out some time," Melissa said.

Jennifer's smile tightened. "Oh, did she? We'll talk about that later."

"But I could learn about being a vet, Mom, and—"

"Melissa…" There was warning in Jennifer's tone, and Barrie glanced between them. It didn't look like Jennifer was on board with this.

"Mom, you said that if a vet were willing to have me around—" Melissa started.

"I said if *Dr. Berton* were willing to have you around," Jennifer said, her gaze flickering toward Barrie and then back to her daughter. "But we couldn't get in to see Dr. Berton, so you'll just have to wait."

Barrie knew exactly what this was about—her pregnancy. Jennifer was a church lady through and through, and this pregnancy offended every sensibility she had. But now was not the time to offend a paying customer. Besides, there was more to Jennifer's story than simply being the mayor's wife and a Sunday school teacher… There was a whole story there that most people didn't know—but Barrie did. She and Jennifer had been close friends when they were fourteen-year-olds in the eighth grade, and when Jennifer disappeared for the rest of the school year, Barrie might have been the only one who knew where she really went.

"It's okay, Melissa," Barrie said. "Dr. Berton is a very nice man."

"But I don't want to go with Dr. Berton," Melissa

said with a shake of her head. "I like Dr. Jones. She's a girl. And she'd know stuff about being a female vet, Mom."

"I said no!" Jennifer cast Barrie a pointed glare. "Could you just leave my daughter alone?"

Jennifer's expression wasn't angry, it was scared, and Barrie understood exactly why. Melissa was her only child…that most people knew about. And this was a delicate situation.

"Why?" Curtis's deep voice reverberated through the room. They both turned to find Curtis standing there, arms crossed over his broad chest, steely gaze trained on Jennifer.

"Excuse me?" Jennifer slammed a hand on her hip and shot him an icy look.

"Why is Barrie such a bad choice?" Curtis asked. "As your daughter pointed out, she's a female vet. She's incredibly good at what she does."

"If you must know, she isn't the kind of influence I want for Melissa. As if that's any of your business."

Melissa blushed pink in embarrassment and Jennifer looked between her vehicle, visible out the window, and Cody, who was starting to wake up a little on the wheeled table. Barrie put a hand on Cody's head and gave him a reassuring stroke.

"Curtis, leave it," Barrie said quietly. He glanced at her, then shook his head.

"She's probably the most moral person in this town," Curtis went on. "So your husband is the mayor, and you think you're better than the rest of us? Sometimes babies happen."

"Curtis—" Barrie repeated, trying to keep her voice moderated. "Shut up!"

Curtis shot her an incredulous look, then shook his head. His expression was one of disgust—but she'd been used to that.

"You're going to accept that?" he retorted. "I've been married to you, and I know firsthand what a Girl Scout you are. You're just going to roll over and accept the scarlet letter with a smile?"

"Mrs. Hartfield is my customer," Barrie retorted, her anger rising. "And as my customer, she is owed a certain level of respect! I don't need you to butt into this, Curtis, so kindly leave it to me!"

Jennifer and Melissa were both watching Barrie and Curtis, and Barrie felt heat rise in her cheeks. She'd *been* in control until Curtis had decided to get all protective of her reputation around here. About fifteen years too late for that! And now she wasn't the smooth-faced professional that she wanted to portray—she was red-faced and fighting with her ex. Nice. This was a delicate situation as it was without Curtis's bumbling attempts to defend her.

"If you could just get the door, Melissa, your mom and I will carry Cody out to your vehicle," Barrie said, forcing a smile.

The girl did as Barrie bid, and Barrie and Jennifer lifted the dog carefully, doing their best not to jostle the leg. He had enough pain killers in him that he should be okay, but still...

As Barrie eased past Curtis, she caught him eyeing her irritably. As if he had any reason to be annoyed!

"Back off, Curtis," she murmured icily. "This is *my* life."

CURTIS WATCHED AS Barrie loaded the dog into the back of the SUV. She moved with confidence and tenderness as she adjusted everything to make sure the animal would be comfortable. That had always softened him—watching her with animals. Something calm and almost angelic radiated from her when she was helping a wounded animal. Everything around her seemed to hush, leaving just her and the creature in her hands. When she turned all her attention on him, it had been like that, too. It was like being in a pool of sunlight when she smiled into his eyes.

But that was long ago, and he'd had to let his fantasies about her go when he was faced with the reality of married life. Being her husband didn't mean that he could bask in that sunlight, because every time he disappointed her, it would turn off, and he'd be more alone than he'd ever been in his life—right next to her.

He'd come by to make peace with her today. He didn't want to leave things like they were after her last visit to the ranch—testy and tense. He'd promised his aunt that he'd be kind, and he was trying to make good on that. Obviously he hadn't done much to repair things, though.

Once the Hartfields' SUV pulled out, Barrie stomped back into the clinic and fixed him with an angry stare.

"What?" he said.

"Did I ask you to jump in and defend my honor?" she snapped. "I had everything well in hand! You're here for, what…a few days…and you think you have any idea of all the tensions around here?"

"Apparently you're one of them," he quipped. "And I'm sorry if I couldn't stand by and have some prissy woman slut-shame you."

"What do you know about my virtue?" she asked, raising one eyebrow. "And how is whoever I sleep with your business?"

So now she was turning this around on him. Curtis barked out a bitter laugh. "I'm in no mood to fight with you. I came by to make peace, but if you're not interested—"

"If I'm not interested, you'll just leave." She shrugged. "Seems like your MO."

"That's not fair." Curtis turned back to her. "I was *defending* you."

"You were making a tense situation even worse," she countered. "Jennifer isn't indignant about me being pregnant out of wedlock. She's scared for her daughter. Jennifer got pregnant in the eighth grade, and her parents pulled her out of school to go have the baby. She gave it up for adoption, and she hadn't even turned fifteen yet. Well, her daughter just turned thirteen, and misguided as her techniques may be, she's trying to make sure that her daughter doesn't end up in the same position."

Curtis blinked. "Jennifer Hartfield?"

"Sunday school teacher, advocate for chastity and purity county-wide…and yes, teenage mother. She wouldn't talk about that baby. She wouldn't say if it was even a boy or a girl, but I knew Jen back then, and giving up her child would have torn her heart out."

He'd never realized that Jen had that kind of tragedy in her past, and he eyed Barrie skeptically as a question rose in his mind.

"How come you never told me that?" he asked.

"I told Jen I'd never breathe a word," Barrie replied.

"I was your husband," Curtis retorted. "And I had more than one run-in with Jen and her high-and-mighty attitude, and you never filled me in…"

What else had she hidden back then? But it had always been like that. Barrie's loyalty was first and foremost to that blasted town!

"What does it matter now?" Barrie shook her head. "I'm trying to keep my clinic together here. So get off your soapbox and butt out of my business. Hope is my home, and you'll drive on out of here in a week or so, but I'm staying. My life is here…my practice is here! So the next time you have the urge to pipe up and put someone in their place—don't!"

Curtis closed his eyes. She didn't need his help. She never had—this town had been her stomping grounds, and she'd always had a better handle on all those conflicting relationships than he ever did. Now he felt stupid standing here…stupid for having thought any of this would change.

"My intentions were sound," he said quietly.

"Just…" She sighed, and didn't finish.

"They always were," he went on. She'd had the last

word—always! But not this time. "You thought I was selfish and egotistical, but everything I did was for you."

"Not anymore," she said.

"Of course not!" He shook his head in exasperation. "We're divorced! I'm putting my own plans first, as I should. What would you have me do, take a hit to make your life easier?"

"I didn't ask you for anything," she snapped.

And standing there, her blue eyes flashing into his, her lips parted as if she were about to come out with another cutting remark, he was reminded so vividly of the old days that he had to hold himself back from shutting her up by kissing her. He knew what those kisses felt like—the softness of her lips, the way her eyes would widen in surprise as he pulled her hard against him...

But this wasn't fifteen years ago, and he wasn't about to do something so stupid as to kiss his ex-wife into silence. Those days were long gone.

"And why do you care if I resent you or not?" she added, turning her back on him as she picked up the cloth that the dog had been lying on.

"I promised my aunt I'd be kind," he said.

"So you're trying to smooth things over for Betty."

"I'm doing it for you!" He was sick of this—the bantering, the constant attempt to get the upper hand. "You might not believe me, Barrie, but I still care about you. I want you to be happy. I want—"

He didn't know how to finish that. He wanted to leave her with a better memory of him than she'd been carrying around for the last fifteen years. He wasn't the same immature kid he used to be, and dumb as it was, he cared how she remembered him.

Barrie slowly turned and eyed him uncertainly. "You care."

"Yeah."

"And you show this by selling my office out from under me."

There it was—she always did have the last word, didn't she?

"I'm heading out," he said, turning for the door. This was why they'd never lasted. She was better in a fight, and she knew how to back him into corners. More than that, he'd stupidly hoped he could be her knight in shining armor. But she had no need for a knight. She took care of her own business—always had. He was the idiot standing off to the side.

Barrie didn't answer him, and he pulled open the door and marched out into the watery winter sunlight.

She'd chosen this town over him back when they were married. She could have come with him on the circuit. It didn't have to be forever. Would a few months have killed her? But this town—and visions of her future inside it—had mattered more to her than an adventure with him. She'd counted on this blasted town to catch her, not him.

He glanced over his shoulder as he headed toward his truck, and he saw Barrie through the window, staring after him. She wasn't angry anymore. She looked like she wanted to cry.

And maybe that was hardest of all, because she didn't need his comfort and he couldn't make things easier on her. Loving Barrie had turned out to be the most painful experience of a lifetime, and he'd be wise to shake those feelings off for good.

Chapter Five

That evening, Curtis came back inside from the last of his chores. His body ached in that pleasurable way that meant he'd put in a hard day's work. He stomped the snow off his boots and shook off his coat.

He'd been thinking about Barrie all day as he worked, and he'd come to a few conclusions—namely, that he was better off taking care of his own affairs and letting her do the same. She was perfectly capable, and if he lost this opportunity to better himself, what solace would it be that his ex-wife had been spared some inconvenience? She'd made herself abundantly clear that morning at her clinic, and he was still stinging from it.

He hung his coat on a peg next to his hat, then paused, standing in the quiet of the house. It was still so much the same—the smells, the one creaky floorboard... This ranch had been a place for transitions in his life: back when he was a teen starting fresh in the country, and now again, starting fresh away from the circuit.

He was still wrapping his mind around his current life changes. Bull riding was the one thing he'd been really good at, and as a bull rider, he knew who he was.

As a joint owner of a stud farm, he'd be nailed down to one piece of land, and if he worked hard enough, he'd have some financial success to lean on. He still didn't know what that would make him, though. Who was he now that he was too old to work the circuit?

Curtis pulled his boots off one by one. The warmth felt good, and the house was scented with freshly baked bread. He clipped his gloves to the clothesline hung above the heat register so they'd dry out before morning.

"Curtis, I was waiting for you to do the honors." Aunt Betty's voice filtered out from the living room.

Curtis headed out of the mudroom and into the kitchen. The leftovers from supper had been put away, but there were still some dinner rolls in a bowl on the counter. He grabbed one and bit into it on his way through to the living room.

The room was softly lit by a couple of lamps and the lights on the Christmas tree. Betty stood next to the window, the curtains drawn.

"Do the honors for what?" Curtis asked as he came in.

"The outside lights. I finished them up this afternoon."

"With your cast?" he asked incredulously. He'd broken an ankle, too—twice, actually—and he knew just how painful that recovery was. He'd wanted his aunt to rest and put that cast up for a couple of weeks. That was why he was here to help her out, after all. The women in this town were notoriously stubborn.

"I didn't push it," she said with a bat of her hand. "But go ahead—flick the switch."

Curtis did as she asked and flicked the switch on the wall next to the front door. Tiny lights wrapped around the top rail of the fence that encircled the yard blazed to life. They were plentiful, like a cloud of fireflies out of season.

"Now it feels like Christmas," Betty said quietly.

"Yeah…it does."

Except this Christmas wasn't just a little break from the ordinary with his aunt. It was a complete break from everything he'd built up to this point in his adult life. He'd always thrived on adventure and change, but this new step, while a change, would give him a completely different lifestyle…something closer to the nailed-down home that Barrie had tried to give him fifteen years ago. And seeing Barrie again had unsettled him, too… She was just as stubborn as she'd always been, so why wasn't he keeping clear of her? He should know better. He had a chance at some success of his own, and he should be enjoying this.

Curtis headed back to the couch and sank into it. From his position, he could see the lights outside glowing in the darkness.

"What's the matter?" Betty asked.

"Hmm?" He roused himself from his thoughts. "Oh, just thinking about the stud farm."

"So why the frown? I thought you wanted this," she said.

He hadn't realized he'd been frowning, and he shrugged. "I do want this. I hate giving up bull riding, is all. But I recognize that I need to sort out something more stable, and this is a great opportunity."

"But it's no eight seconds," Betty concluded.

He chuckled. "It's no eight seconds," he agreed.

"Not everything worthwhile risks your hide," Betty said.

"I know," he said with a quick grin. "Like making some good money. If I can't ride bulls, I'll settle for a lucrative income. This stud farm is already performing well."

"What does your mom think of all this?" Betty asked. "Have you talked to her lately?"

"I texted with her last night," he admitted.

"And?" Betty's tone seemed a little too carefully indifferent. The sisters were as different as night and day. Both women cared about each other, even if they didn't understand each other. And when it came to Curtis, they both were protective of him in their own ways. It was like being stuck between a rock and a hard place, except the rock and the hard place were slightly judgmental of each other.

"You know Mom," he said. "She can appreciate a fresh start."

His mother had thrown her life into a struggling singing career, so she was the one person who could fully understand his adrenaline junkie ways.

"What's she doing for Christmas?" Betty asked.

"She has a singing gig at a local country club."

"At her age." Betty shook her head.

"She's fifty-four," he countered.

Betty raised her eyebrows as if nothing else needed to be said, and Curtis shook his head. His mom had aged well, so while she was in her fifties, she could pass for her midforties, and she could sing a country ballad that could break a heart in two. Sure, she hadn't gotten her big break, and maybe never would, but there were plenty of singers who made some money on the side doing what they loved, and Noreen Porter was one of them.

The fact that his mother had sent him to Betty's ranch in the first place spoke of just how desperate Noreen had been, because going to Betty for help would have given her pride a hit.

"She's not alone, if that's what you're worried about," Curtis added with a short laugh.

"What's his name?" Betty asked.

"Scott. He seems to be a nice guy."

Betty raised an eyebrow, then shrugged. "I shouldn't judge. As long as she's happy."

Betty didn't mean that, and Curtis knew it, but he appreciated her saying it anyway. His mom had worked through a fair number of men in her life, and Betty... hadn't.

"But what about you, Aunty?" Curtis asked, moving the conversation away from his mother. "Any guys in your life?"

"Just the bovine variety." Betty's gaze turned toward the window and the twinkling lights along the fence.

"You obviously know a few human males," he pressed.

"Several." Betty shot him a smart-alecky look, and he laughed.

"Any of them remotely your age and single?"

"Nope. Married. Every last one." She paused, then

pressed her lips together. "Well, except for one. But he's widowed, so it's just about the same thing."

This was new. Curtis far preferred needling his aunt about her personal life to listening to her gripe about his mother. "Who is he?"

"Dr. Berton."

Curtis sobered. The man who was seriously considering buying that commercial building from him. He'd been intending to tease his aunt about a possible romance, but Curtis hadn't realized that Palmer Berton's wife had passed away, and the humor seeped out of the moment.

"What happened to Louise? I didn't realize she'd died."

"It was a brain aneurysm last summer," Betty replied. "Very fast and tragic. Like I said, it's the same thing as being married. Berton is still grieving."

Palmer and Louise had been a fixture around Hope. They had two sons, both in the army.

"He never mentioned Louise passing when we talked about the sale," Curtis said.

"He wouldn't," Betty replied. "He's private that way. He keeps his grief to himself."

"He talks to you, though," Curtis said. She seemed to know a fair bit about how he grieved, at the very least.

"Sure, we talk. Sometimes people need someone to talk to, especially after a loss like that. I've known Palmer since we were kids, and he's been my primary vet ever since I inherited this place," Betty said. "We have history."

There was so much history in this town that Curtis

had never guessed, but people born and raised here—like Barrie—were connected to the rest of Hope at the roots. Curtis had always seen himself as an outsider in Hope, but he had his own history here, entwined with a woman who still drove him nuts.

"You still think Dr. Berton will use the building to push Barrie out of business?" he asked.

"Louise gave him balance," Betty said. "She tempered his more aggressive nature. And now that she's gone, he's got a lot of time on his hands that he'll be putting into his work. It's only natural."

Curtis sighed. "Do you have any clout with him?"

Betty shot Curtis a sharp look. "Having second thoughts about that sale?"

"No." He sucked in a deep breath. "If I don't sell that building, I've got nothing. I might not like it, but that's a fact. I just wish it could be smoother…for everyone."

For Barrie. That's what he meant. He wished his step forward didn't have to impact her quite so much. He wished all of this were simpler and he could arrange a sale and walk away without any nagging guilt. The shared histories in a small ranching community weren't always a comfort.

"Some Christmas…" Curtis said after a few beats of silence.

"It might not be a merry Christmas for all of us," Betty said softly. "But Christmas comes all the same."

True enough. Dr. Berton was widowed, Betty had a broken ankle, Barrie was pregnant and facing her first Christmas without her mother… Here Curtis was in Hope, working alongside his pregnant ex-wife, who he'd never really gotten over, making her life more difficult in order to scrape a future together for himself. It wasn't exactly a merry Christmas, but Christmas came once a year whether they were in the mood for it or not.

THE NEXT MORNING, Barrie pushed Miley's face away from her shoulder and turned her vehicle onto the Porter ranch drive. This would be a busy day. She had the Porter cows to check on, then a visit to the Granger ranch, where she had some calves to immunize. The truck had given her some trouble starting that morning, and she couldn't even blame the cold. Fourteen degrees wasn't exactly balmy, but it wasn't cold enough to shut down a vehicle, either.

She'd been thinking about her mother a lot lately. She hadn't been gone long, and this Christmas loomed. It wasn't just the thought of merriment without Mom. It was all the questions she wouldn't be able to ask her, all the advice she'd miss out on. Until she got pregnant, she hadn't realized how much she still desperately needed to be mothered herself.

Mom would have had something to say about Curtis's reappearance, and she wished her mother were here to say it all. "Love is one thing, Barrie. And being man enough to take care of a family is another. You can love a man heart and soul and still not be able to live with him."

That was what her mother had said a few weeks before Curtis took off. She'd said it again in the weeks that followed. Love wasn't enough… Somehow, it had given her permission to let go of him. It didn't mean she hadn't loved him, it just meant it hadn't worked. But now he was back, and she found herself unsettled about the muscular cowboy. She needed her mother's wisdom to set her straight. Gwyneth Jones had always had an uncanny ability to see through the smoke screen and get right down to basics.

"I love you, but I need some personal space, Miley," she said, and Miley snuffled at her ear instead of obeying. She nudged his nose back again as she followed the drive around and pulled up in front of the house. She gave a short beep of the horn to let Betty know that she was here, and Betty emerged a moment later in the doorway, a sweater pulled around her shoulders. Barrie lowered her window.

"Dr. Jones!" Betty called with a smile, hobbling up to the driver's side. "Curtis is down in the barn already, so you might as well drive through."

"Thanks." Barrie raised her voice over the sound of her truck's engine. "I'll keep you posted on the situation down there."

"Sounds good," Betty replied, and she gave a final wave before she disappeared back into the house. Barrie put the truck in gear and hit the button to put up the window. It was cold out there, and she cranked the steering wheel to head down the drive toward the barn.

Why couldn't seeing Curtis again be easier? She hadn't meant to give him any kind of reaction yesterday. That had happened on its own, and she'd regretted it. It showed weakness. She'd made it seem like she hadn't dealt with their divorce, when she had. How many hours had she and Mom talked it out? Barrie had made her peace with having done her very best, and it not being enough. That hadn't been easy. But seeing him again had opened a few old wounds.

Why couldn't he have lost some of that magnetism with age? That would have been more fair. He'd come back to town to find her single and pregnant. At the very least, he could have come back with a bald spot and a pot belly to match the other guys from their class. But having him be all gentle and sweet with her out there in the field was irritating. Having him standing up for her as if she needed the pity was even worse. If it weren't for her pregnancy, would Curtis still be this sweet? Not likely. She didn't need his special treatment.

The red of the barn's sides contrasted with the snow on its roof. Icicles hung off the eaves, glittering in morning sunlight. She liked these early morning rounds, at least when she wasn't going to be running into Curtis. But she had a job to do, and her practice needed the income. She couldn't afford to recommend that Curtis call in Palmer Berton just to give herself some space.

Barrie parked in front of the barn's main doors and hopped out of the truck. She opened up the back door and Miley poured himself out of the back seat, then gave himself a shake, his tags jingling.

"Come on, Miley," she said, giving the dog's head a stroke. Then she pulled open the passenger side door and grabbed her vet's bag. "You be good now, okay?"

But Miley knew the drill. When Barrie opened the barn door, Miley followed her in, his head staying by her side. She let her eyes adjust, then scanned the barn. She spotted Curtis near the back. He was leaning over a rail, looking into a stall, his face in the shadows. She knew that stance—she couldn't see his feet, but she could tell he'd hooked a boot over the bottom rail. He straightened and tipped his hat.

"Morning," she called.

"Morning." He pulled off his gloves. "Two more quarantined since last night."

Barrie nodded. "Four in total now?"

"That's right."

Miley's nails clicked against the concrete floor as Barrie headed down the aisle toward the back of the barn, where Curtis waited. She had antibiotics to administer and temperatures to take. The baby shifted, and she gave the side of her belly a rub. The movements were getting stronger as the weeks passed, and she could feel a good hard jab to the bladder now and again. That was irritating when she wasn't near a washroom, but it was also reassuring. If her baby could wake her up several times a night with wriggles and stretches, then all was well—at least in the baby's world. The outside world was a little more complex.

When she arrived at the stall where Curtis waited, Barrie pointed to the floor.

"Miley, lie down," she said. Miley complied, his eyes fixed on her. "Any improvement with the first calf?" she asked, turning to Curtis. He'd shaved since she'd seen him yesterday, and he held a pair of gloves loosely in one hand, his shirt sleeves rolled up to reveal muscular forearms. He was definitely a more solid man now—the years had hardened him in a way she'd find appealing if she didn't know him better.

"He seems to be getting better," Curtis said. "He's eating more and he's less lethargic."

Both good signs. She turned her attention to the newest quarantined cows and inspected them with an expert eye. She let herself into the first stall and opened her bag. She wasn't wasting any time here this morning—the Grangers were waiting.

"Last night I found out that Louise Berton passed away," Curtis said, and Barrie glanced up.

"This year. She had an aneurysm," she confirmed. "Mom died in February, and then Louise passed in June."

"It's been a tough year," he said.

Barrie turned her attention back to the calf. She pulled out a syringe and the antibiotic. "Miserable."

There had been no warning when her mother died. Dad came back from work and found Mom on the floor. He called an ambulance, but when they got her to the hospital, they'd pronounced her already gone. One day, Mom was her usual bright, funny self. And then... Barrie blinked back a mist of tears. The pain was still fresh.

Curtis was silent while Barrie administered the medication and rubbed the spot to relieve the sting. She pushed herself to her feet, then took her bag and headed to the next stall over. Miley raised his head.

"Stay," she commanded.

"How are you holding up?" Curtis asked.

"If I say that I'm fine, you'll say I'm lying," she said as she squatted next to the other calf. "And if I say I'm not fine, what are you going to do about it?"

Curtis sighed. "I'm still not allowed to care?"

"No. You aren't. You lost that right when you left me."

"I'm sorry that your mom is gone, all the same," he said. "Your mom might not have thought I was right for you, but she was a good person."

Her mom was more than a good person. She'd been a great mom, too. She'd been full of advice and hard-won wisdom. She'd been a silent listener when necessary, and a ferocious ally. She'd made the best shortbread cookies and decorated them for every single occasion possible from Christmas to baby showers. She'd even made Barrie some postdivorce cookies—pink hearts with icing Band-Aids.

"It'll get better, Barrie," her mother had told her.

"What makes you so sure?" Barrie had asked bitterly. *"You've never been divorced."*

"I don't have to know divorce," Gwyneth had retorted. *"I know my daughter. And you're strong and beautiful. You'll get through this. Life is long, and you have so much more ahead of you..."*

Barrie administered the shot, then rose to her feet. She glanced over to find Curtis still watching her.

"Betty's worried about you," he said.

Somehow that got past her defenses. Maybe because Betty was close to her mom's age...

"And Betty is allowed to worry," she snapped. "You know why? Because she's a friend and a customer. She's a part of my life. You aren't anymore. You didn't want this life, this town...or *me*. You made your choice. Do I resent you? A bit. But that doesn't mean you have anything to fix or make right. I have a job to do. So do you. Let's just keep it on those lines."

Barrie opened the stall door, and Curtis took a step back to let her out. He didn't retreat further than one stride to allow the gate to swing open, however. He closed the clasp on the gate and she shot him a cool smile, then slid past him toward the stalls of the other two cows that were recovering. Miley rose to his feet, clicked over to the stall where she was working and sat down on his haunches. Barrie administered the antibiotics quickly, checked the calves' vitals and was pleased to see some improvement.

When she let herself out of the last stall, she found Curtis eyeing her with a thoughtful look on his face.

"What?" she asked testily. She'd told herself that she'd be professional and contained this time, but there was something about Curtis's attention that irritated her.

"It's nice to see you again, that's all."

His thorough appraisal made her skin tingle. He'd always had that effect on her, but she wasn't dumb enough to succumb to it anymore.

"Let me ask you this. If I weren't pregnant, would you feel this way?"

"What way?"

"Whatever this is." She shrugged. "This urge to make sure I'm okay. You've always had far too much testosterone coursing through your veins, and that factored into all of our problems. But right now, you aren't reacting to *me*. You're reacting to my belly. I'm no longer Barrie, the woman who drove you nuts. I'm now… this…" She spread her arms. "Curtis, it's still me. We don't have anything to sort out. Our marriage is history. I'm the vet. You have sick cows. It's pretty simple."

Barrie patted her thigh and Miley rose to his feet and immediately tagged along after her. When he got to her side, the dog cast a mournful look back at Curtis, and Barrie grit her teeth. Even the dog was softening to that frustrating man! She reached over and gave Miley's head a scratch all the same. The poor dog couldn't be blamed for his good temper.

Barrie pushed open the door and headed out into the bright sunlight. She tossed her vet's bag onto the passenger side front seat, then opened the back door to let Miley up. He clambered onto the seat, and she slammed the door.

How did Curtis Porter always manage to get under her skin like that? Why did she even allow him to bother her? They were ancient history. They'd never had children together. There was nothing tying them to each other, save a few memories. But then he'd look at her in that way he had, and she'd see red. It was stupid. She knew it.

As she angled around to the driver's side and let herself in, Miley was still scrambling about, trying to get comfortable. Barrie put the key into the ignition and turned it. There was a grinding sound, but the engine didn't turn over.

"Blast." She shut her eyes, willing the engine to cooperate, then turned the key again. Nothing.

She sighed and looked back at Miley. Miley whined and gave a low growl—his form of commiseration—and she ran her hand through her hair. For all of her bravado back there in the barn, all she wanted was to get out of here—get onto open road, away from him.

"One more try," she muttered, and turned the key again, but instead of hearing the engine, there was a tap on her window. She grimaced, then glanced over to see Curtis. Her plans to be through with the man as quickly as possible seemed to be slipping through her fingers. She lowered the window.

"You have a problem there?" he asked.

She sighed. "It won't start. I'll call a tow."

"Want me to take a look?" he asked.

"Since when do you fix trucks?" she demanded. "You rode bulls. You were no mechanic."

They weren't here to reinvent history, or for him to play hero. Whatever he had on his conscience, he'd have to sort out without her.

Curtis crossed his arms over his chest. "So what's the plan, then?"

"I'll get towed to the garage," she said. "And I'll have to call the Grangers and tell them I can't make it."

"So you have another call," Curtis clarified. He looked away for a moment, chewing the side of his cheek, then back at her. "What if I drove you?"

"To the Grangers'?" She frowned. "Why?"

"Why not?" he shot back. "Do you need a reason? How about guilt? I'm selling that building out from under you and I feel like I owe you something. Is that reason enough?"

It was the most honest thing she'd heard from him yet. She couldn't afford to be sending business to Palmer Berton, and a ride would allow her to do her job while she waited for a mechanic to fix her truck.

Barrie eyed him for a moment, then nodded. "Alright. Thanks. I'd appreciate the ride."

He was right; he did owe her.

Chapter Six

Curtis stepped back as Barrie pushed open the door and slid slowly to the ground. He hadn't been sure if she'd accept his offer of help, but he was glad she had. His aunt's ranch wasn't too far from the Granger ranch. Besides, there was a part of him that didn't want to see her leave. It was a stupid part of him, but it was still there. Barrie had always drawn him in like that, whether it was good for him or not.

Barrie's pregnancy slowed her movements, but right now he knew better than to offer her a hand. She wasn't about to let him in close, and he couldn't entirely blame her. She was right—fifteen years was a long time, and he wasn't a part of her life anymore. What *was* he feeling for her, exactly?

Barrie adjusted her jacket over her hips, and he refused to allow himself to appreciate how well her jeans fit. She'd always been slender when he'd known her, but pregnancy had rounded her from behind as well. Was she right—was he reacting to her pregnancy or to her as a woman? Because she *had* driven him crazy back then...

Barrie circled around her stalled SUV for her black
bag, and opened the back door. The dog unfolded himself and scrambled down to the ground. That was one
huge dog. He stood as tall as a colt, and stayed protectively close to his mistress.

"We'll walk up to my truck at the house," Curtis said.
"You okay with that?"

"I'm fine," she said. "I'd better call a tow truck,
though."

Curtis waited while she dialed the local towing company, and within a couple of minutes, she'd given the
crucial information.

"Alright," she said as she hung up. "Let's go."

So competent—not that she shouldn't be, but even
though she'd accepted his offer of a ride, he had the feeling that she didn't really need his favors. Miley trotted
next to Barrie, but when Curtis fell into step on the other
side, Miley fell back for a pace, then nudged between
them, the warm bulk of his shoulder shoving Curtis
over. The dog was definitely making a statement here.

"Miley doesn't like me?" Curtis asked with a short
laugh.

Barrie looked down at Miley, then shrugged. "If he
didn't like you, you'd know it."

What did that mean exactly? He wasn't sure he
wanted to find out. The Great Dane was a friendly
enough breed, but Miley was still two hundred pounds
of solid muscle. They found their stride as they headed
up the road toward the house, and after a couple of minutes of walking, Miley seemed to lose interest in protecting his mistress and bounded ahead.

"Traitor." Barrie chuckled.

"Is he a good guard dog?" Curtis asked.

"He's awful," she replied. "You can buy him off for a treat."

Curtis shrugged his coat higher on his neck to fend off the probing cold. "He makes a good impression, though."

"Which is why I keep him around." The old joking glint was back in her eyes, despite the lack of a smile on her face. She walked at a brisker pace than he expected, but then, she was used to marching through fields to find injured cattle, so this was nothing, even with her pregnancy.

"So, what's your history with Palmer?" Curtis asked.

"I told you. I worked for him for a few years before I started my own practice."

"Betty told me you're the better vet," he said.

Barrie shot him a quizzical look. "Why would she say that?"

"She says he's more experienced, but you have better instincts," he replied. "She says that he's peaked in his career, and you're still climbing."

"Not that Dr. Berton would ever admit it," she quipped.

"So you didn't work well together," he said.

"He was a micromanager. He wanted me to do everything his way, not mine. I'm a good vet—Betty's right. I don't know…" She sighed. "I thought he'd be glad to get rid of me when I opened my own practice, but he was furious. He said I was ungrateful."

"Maybe he recognized the competition," Curtis suggested.

Barrie shrugged. "Maybe."

She'd always been talented. Barrie didn't do anything unless she could be the best at it, and when he knew her, she'd never taken anything less than seriously. Curtis was different, though. He liked to go with the flow for the most part, and his competitive streak only came out in the bull riding. For all the good that had done him.

"So you butted heads a lot, I take it," Curtis clarified.

"He wouldn't trust my way of doing things," she replied. "I have the same education he does—more current, even. But that's Dr. Berton for you—it's his way or the highway."

"You want to know what I think?" he asked with a small smile.

"I'm not sure I do," she retorted.

"I think Aunt Betty might be sweet on him."

Barrie's attitude evaporated and she looked at him in shock. "What?"

There she was—the Barrie he remembered. He felt a surge of satisfaction at having shocked her into a more natural reaction. He knew he shouldn't be gossiping about his aunt, but it felt good to get past the icy veneer.

"Hey, I'm not saying it's a fact. Just a…feeling, I guess. They're friends. So don't pass that around."

"Your aunt has better taste than that," Barrie replied, but her tone had warmed.

"They're both single, and the same age," he countered. "I always thought Betty would have liked to get married. She just never seemed to find the right cowboy."

"So that's why she never married?" Barrie asked. "Just bad luck?"

"Or bad timing." Curtis shrugged. "And there could be worse matches."

"He's impossible," Barrie countered.

"You're impossible, Curtis!" How many times had she muttered that over the course of their short marriage? And he felt a strange urge to stick up for Dr. Berton in spite of it all.

"He was married for what…thirty-five years?" Curtis raised his eyebrows. "Louise handled him. And if Betty can wrangle cattle, I don't see Palmer being too much for her."

"Some cowboys aren't worth the trouble," she retorted.

And he was obviously one of them. But he'd won her over once… Her refusal to deal with difficult cowboys shouldn't be sparking up his competitive streak. He pushed the thought firmly away.

Miley came bounding back toward them in joyful abandon. While Curtis had ridden bulls in the ring, he still found this massive dog slightly unsettling. At least a man knew a bull's intentions, and he could brace himself for it. Miley's jowls flapped with each leap. Barrie cracked a smile for the first time that morning as Miley fell into step next to her again—standing solidly between Curtis and her mistress.

"You're back, are you?" she asked the dog, stroking his head, which came up to her chest.

Miley turned to look at Curtis, and he could have sworn he saw a challenge in the dog's eyes. Or was that his imagination?

Curtis's truck was parked in front of the house. As they approached, Betty poked her head out of the screen door. While Barrie went over to talk to Betty, Curtis sauntered over to his truck and started clearing out the back. Normally the back seat wasn't put to use, but that dog was going to need all of it. He covered the leather seats with a woolen blanket, tucking it in at the headrests. It would have to do.

Soon enough, Barrie returned with Miley at her side, and Curtis opened both doors—one for Barrie and one for Miley. The dog hesitated, watching his mistress.

"Let's go, Miley," Barrie said. "Get in."

Miley did as he was told, and Curtis inwardly grimaced at the sound of dog toenails against leather seats as the blanket was pushed aside. He slammed the door. He held out his hand for Barrie, and she gave him her bag of veterinarian supplies and carefully hoisted herself up into the passenger seat. Then she reached for her bag.

"You are one stubborn woman, Barrie," he said with a short laugh.

"One of my many strengths."

And looking at her life now, maybe she was right, because his way hadn't exactly panned out. He swung her door shut and headed to the driver's side. When he hopped into the truck and started the vehicle, he heard panting close behind his head, and he glanced back to see Miley staring him in the face.

"Hello, Miley," Curtis said uncertainly. "Want to sit back a bit?"

"Miley," Barrie said reproachfully. "Personal space!"

The dog retreated a few inches, but the smell of dog breath was still rather close. Curtis pulled out of his parking spot and headed down the drive that led to the main road.

"He's a bit of a back seat driver," Barrie said, adjusting her bag on her lap. "Thanks for doing this, Curtis. I appreciate it."

"What do the Grangers need?" he asked.

"I'm doing some calf immunizations," she replied. "We've had this appointment scheduled for a couple of weeks now, and it takes some preparation to get the calves all in the barn, so canceling would be a real headache for them..."

And as she talked about the different types of immunizations and the reasons behind them, Curtis noticed Miley's gray face creeping up next to his once more. Curtis looked over, and his face connected with the dog's jowls. He planted a hand on Miley's nose and pushed him back.

"Miley..." Barrie reprimanded him. "Go back! Now!"

Miley retreated once more with a low growl that sounded more like a complaint than a threat, and Curtis started to laugh. It was ridiculous—this massive dog that wanted to be as close as possible to the humans around him.

Curtis eased to a stop at the main road.

"Miley!" Curtis commanded. "Come here." The

dog's face appeared over his shoulder again, and Curtis gave him a thorough scratch behind the ears. "You're a good boy," he reassured the dog. "Aren't you?"

Miley cocked his head from side to side to get the best pet possible, and when he was through, he retreated on his own. There was the scramble of toenails against seat as he got comfortable once more. Barrie was looking at Curtis in surprise, and he ignored her.

Curtis signaled his turn and pulled onto the main road. As he looked both ways, he caught Barrie watching him still, her expression softened, less guarded.

"I'm a nicer guy than you think," he said, his voice low.

There was a beat of silence as he accelerated a little past the speed limit.

"I know," she said with a sigh.

"Are you agreeing with me?" He shot her a surprised look.

"Of course. You're a nice guy, and you do mean well. I don't think you're some heartless SOB trying to till me under. I never thought that. You put up this tough front, but under it all you have a lot of heart." She paused. "I never should have married you, though."

That stung—not quite the reaction he'd expected. "Okay…"

"You know what I mean," she said. "You aren't the devil, Curtis. And neither am I. We just want different things—always have. We never should have run off to Rickton and eloped. That was the biggest mistake we ever made."

"You really regret what we had that much?" he asked.

Because he didn't. She was still his biggest adventure to date.

She sighed. "I regret having to get over you, Curtis. That was misery."

Had it been that hard on her? He'd wondered over the years. It had been agony for him—starting fresh, his heart in shreds. It had taken him two years to ask another woman out, even with all the girls willing to throw themselves at him on the circuit.

"What do you mean?" he asked cautiously, not even sure he wanted to hear this, but he probably should. He'd had an effect on her, and he should take some responsibility for it.

"Lying in bed at night—our bed—and knowing you weren't coming back." There was a tremor in her voice. "Or the day I packed away that white summer dress I wore for our wedding. I know I said I wanted a dress I could wear again, but how could I? I'd married you in that dress. Or facing the onslaught of questions from everyone who wanted to know where you'd gone. And I had to tell them that you'd left. We were over."

"Did you tell them you kicked me out?" he asked.

"Of course." She laughed bitterly. "I had to save face."

He was silent, her words rattling around inside him. He'd hurt her more deeply than he'd suspected. He'd always imagined that he'd left her behind furious. Maybe it was easier for him to think of her as angry instead of gutted.

"It was bad for me, too," he admitted gruffly. But he didn't want to enlarge on that. He'd had his own sleepless nights, and it had taken him a few weeks to finally take off his wedding ring...

"So we're agreed," she said.

"That I'm not the devil?" He shot her a wry look.

She smiled faintly, then rolled her eyes. Back when he was nothing more than a kid, he'd loved the challenge of winning her heart, and while he wasn't the same naive sap he used to be, there was still a small part of him that liked the challenge of changing her opinion about him.

"Yeah, we're agreed," he said after a minute.

He was a nicer guy than she thought. He stood by that. But she was right—they never should have married to begin with. That divorce had been both inevitable and the worst pain he'd ever endured.

THE GRANGER RANCH was about thirty minutes away from the Porter land, and by the time they arrived, Miley was antsy in the back seat. Curtis was more patient with her dog than Barrie had thought he'd be, and she had to admit that had softened her a little toward her ex-husband—very little. And she was grudgingly grateful to him for taking her to this appointment with the Grangers.

They parked beside the Grangers' house. The twin boys, who were about three years old now, were playing outside in the snow, and Mackenzie was standing in the window with the baby on her shoulder. She waved and disappeared from the window, and a moment later the side door opened. She still had the baby on her shoulder, but there was a blanket over the baby's head now to protect her from the chill.

"Hi, Barrie!" Mack called. "Where's your truck?"

"It broke down at the Porter ranch. Curtis kindly offered to shuttle me around this morning," she replied. Mackenzie Granger was one of the few people who hadn't been around during Barrie and Curtis's short marriage, and for that, Barrie was grateful. She was tired of dodging explanations. "Should I just head down to the barn?"

"I'll text Chet and Andy to tell them you're here," Mack replied. "But yes—just head on down. Thanks, Barrie." She turned her attention to the boys in the snow. "Jayden, no snow in the face!"

"Mack!" Barrie leaned out the window again. "Which barn?"

"The Granger barn." Mackenzie grinned. "Sorry, I should have specified."

Barrie waved and put her window back up. Curtis eased the truck forward and raised his eyebrows.

"Which barn is that?"

"Just follow the road down," Barrie said. "It's the first one."

Mack had her hands full with three kids now, and Barrie felt a wave of anxiety. She'd be the mom with a new baby soon enough, but she wasn't as ready for all of this as Mackenzie had been. Mack was in a solid, supportive marriage to a great guy. She owned half this ranch, and there was a certain amount of freedom that came with that, too.

Barrie was still grieving for her own mom, and while

she'd always wanted children, she'd envisioned that happening with her mother in her life.

The truck bounced over a rut, and Barrie winced, bracing herself.

"Sorry," Curtis said. "Didn't see that one coming."

"It's okay…" But the more her pregnancy progressed, the more painful jolts like that got. Curtis slowed down and eased around a pothole.

"So that's Chet's wife?" Curtis asked.

"Yes. Mackenzie is Helen Vaughn's granddaughter. I don't know if Betty told you, but she passed away a few years back and left Mack the ranch. She and Chet got married and joined their ranches. It's a profitable outfit."

"Strange to see old buddies with families and kids."

"Andy is Chet's ranch manager," Barrie added.

"Chet's brother, Andy? I thought he was in the city."

"No, he came back. He ended up marrying Dakota Mason—Brody's sister."

Curtis shook his head. "Wow. Time marches on."

It did, indeed. Barrie rubbed a hand over her belly. This was the easy part, she'd been told. Pregnancy was hard, but once a newborn was in the world, everything would be infinitely more complicated. She wouldn't have the luxury of staying home with her baby like Mackenzie did, and her heart ached at the thought of handing her newborn over to someone else while she went tramping out into fields as the local vet. She had no safety net to catch her, which was a position she shared with a lot of hardworking women.

The Granger barn was down a sloping road that bent west, within sight of the Vaughn barn. That was a vestige from the days when people wanted their neighbors within shouting distance. It made sense, because emergencies came up, and people needed each other. It was a simpler time. Before the two ranches were joined, a fence had separated the barns. But that fence had been torn down when Chet and Mack got married, and the two barns were both put to use.

The truck rumbled to a stop next to a rusted blue pickup. Barrie eased herself down to the ground and opened the back door to let Miley out.

"Come on, Miley," she said. The dog hopped down, his long legs reaching the ground more easily than she had, and stretched. Curtis came around the truck just as she grabbed her black bag. A few yards off, a white goat regarded them cautiously.

"Don't even think about it, Miley," Barrie warned. "You stay put."

The barn door opened, and Andy Granger stuck his head out. "Butter Cream, you little scamp. Get back in."

The goat sauntered lazily toward the door, gave one backward glance at the new arrivals and disappeared inside.

"Curtis Porter? Is that you, man?" Andy asked, turning his attention to them.

Curtis headed over and the two men shook hands. They'd been friends in high school.

"Are you two—" Andy hooked a thumb in Barrie's direction, and Barrie lifted one eyebrow. The inference was obvious. As much as she liked being talked about in front of her face, rather than behind her back, she had no patience left for the curiosity of this town.

"Curtis is my ride today," Barrie said with a small smile. "And I'm your vet. Shall we?"

Andy chuckled and shook his head. "Hey, at least I'm the kind of guy who asks instead of gossiping with the neighbors."

Barrie laughed. "I'll give you that. But there's nothing to wonder about. Curtis is back in town long enough to sell the building I'm leasing. Then he's leaving."

"Oh, yeah?" Andy shot Curtis a questioning look. "You have something going on?"

"I'm buying a stud farm with a business partner," Curtis replied.

"Have you seen anyone else from the old days?" Andy asked as they headed toward the barn door.

"Not really planning on sticking around for a reunion," Curtis said with a short laugh. "Are any of the guys still in town?"

"A few."

"Whatever happened to Dwight Petersen?" Curtis asked. Andy frowned, then caught Barrie's eye.

"Drank himself into oblivion," Barrie answered for him. "You can find him at the Honky Tonk pretty much any day of the week."

"Anyone try to help him out?" Curtis asked.

"Who hasn't?" Andy replied. "I've personally driven him to AA several times, but it never seems to stick. People have pretty much given up." Andy pulled open the barn door. "Fifteen years changes a lot."

Barrie had to admit that Andy had probably tried harder than most people to get Dwight some help, which was magnanimous considering the history his wife, Dakota, had with the guy. But Dwight was one of those people who, faced with two choices, would pick the wrong one every time.

Andy went into the barn first, and Curtis held the door for Barrie. She glanced up as she passed in front of him, the faint smell of musk tickling her nose. His dark gaze followed her, and he moved in close behind her as the door shut. Andy moved on ahead, and Curtis's hand pressed against the small of her back, nudging her forward. She could feel the warmth emanating from his body, and his touch softened, turned more gentle and pliant...

She knew that touch... Her breath caught, and she shut her eyes for a moment, pushing back her familiar physical response. Why couldn't fifteen years have changed *that*? She missed those warm touches, the smell of his cologne.

"Don't do that," she murmured, glancing back.

"Do what?" His dark eyes glittered in the low light, and her heart gave a flutter. His hand was still on her back, warm and solid.

"That. Be all gentlemanly."

She had no right to miss him. He belonged in the past, and she'd worked too hard to get where she was to let herself romanticize a doomed relationship. Like Andy said, fifteen years changed a lot around here.

Curtis's warm touch dropped away. "Sorry about that. Habit, I guess."

Habit... They'd had a good long time to break those habits, but she understood what he meant. Curtis coming back seemed to conflate the time in some ways, bring back memories so solidly that they ached.

She picked up her pace and sucked in a deep, stabilizing breath. She'd rather do this job without Curtis here to distract her, but she'd take what she could right now.

The barn was warm and smelled of tangy hay. The white goat, Butter Cream, was now in a stall with a couple of new kids. The low moo of weaned calves echoed against the walls, and Barrie followed Andy's lead toward the west side of the barn. Dakota was waiting, filling feed pails for the calves. When she turned toward them, Barrie was surprised at how large her belly had become. Petite Dakota was pregnant, too, but much further along. She was carrying the baby all in front, it seemed.

"Barrie!" Dakota shot her a grin. "Look at you! I haven't seen you since you started to show. How far along are you now?"

Barrie glanced down at her own belly—much smaller than her friend's.

"About five months," she replied. "You?"

"Eight months. Ready to be done with this already." She looked tired and a little wan.

Andy arrived at his wife's side and reached for the pail of feed she held. Dakota shot him a look of warning. "I've got it, Andy. I'm fine."

Andy put his hands up in retreat. "Just trying to help."

"I don't *need* help," Dakota snapped. Then her cheeks flushed. "Sorry, I'm testy."

"She is," Andy confirmed. "But since I contributed to this pregnancy, I still keep trying to help."

Andy grinned at his wife, and Dakota looked ready to smack him. It was the hormones—Barrie could recognize that straight away. Barrie was feeling the same way—irritable and ready to lambaste whoever tried to help her out. She knew it wasn't a wise approach, but she couldn't seem to help herself, either. Wasn't motherhood supposed to soften her? Instead she was getting more frustrated, and the only way to make herself feel better was to prove that she didn't need extra help. Judging from Dakota's reaction, maybe she wasn't alone in that.

Andy and Curtis moved off to check some of the new calves, leaving the women in privacy.

"So… Curtis?" Dakota asked quietly as Barrie set down her bag and opened it.

"Your husband already asked," Barrie said with a bitter laugh. She pulled out some syringes and the bottles of vaccine fluid. "There's nothing to tell. He's selling the building I'm leasing and then leaving town. He feels like he owes me something. And he does."

Dakota eyed her questioningly. "Is he the father?"

Barrie rolled her eyes. "No, he's not the father. He's just the idiot ex-husband who's going to sell my office space to Palmer Berton."

"Ouch." Dakota shook her head. "'Idiot' is right."

Barrie sighed. Except she could grudgingly understand why he was doing it—it just wasn't convenient for her right now. But this pregnancy was her own fault…

well, hers and the married vet who wanted nothing to do with her.

"Andy's driving you crazy, is he?" Barrie asked.

"Oh, I'm going nuts…" Dakota sighed. "He keeps trying to take things out of my hands, or he'll hand me little bites of food like I'm a squirrel or something—" She gritted her teeth. "It sounds stupid when I say it, but I feel huge, and my hormones are soaring and…"

"Yeah, I get it." Barrie chuckled. "He's a good guy, though."

"I didn't say I don't *love* him," Dakota said with a shake of her head. "I just want to kill him half the time. I really hope this improves once the baby arrives, because I don't know how much longer he'll be able to stand me."

Barrie looked over to where Curtis and Andy stood together. Andy's gentle green-eyed gaze was focused on his wife. Curtis's dark gaze drilled into Barrie. He wasn't flirting or teasing—she was well accustomed to both with Curtis. This was a different look, something slightly guarded but filled with painful longing. Her heart sped up, and she swallowed, breaking the eye contact.

"Andy still seems pretty smitten to me," Barrie said.

"You sure Curtis's only here to sell that property?" Dakota asked softly.

Barrie sighed. "I'm positive. We aren't all as lucky as you are."

Except that look he'd given her—he missed all of this, too. She knew better than to think it changed a single thing, but whatever it was that had drawn them together in the first place hadn't gone away.

Barrie pulled her attention back to the job at hand. None of them had time to waste. This ranch wouldn't run itself, and neither would the Porter ranch.

"Okay, so let's get started," Barrie said. "I've got the first vaccines ready. Let's begin with this stall here, and we'll work our way back."

For Barrie, doing her job helped to soothe that rising anxiety inside her. She might not know how to balance everything as a single mother, but she did know how to give animals medical care. Sometimes it helped to just stick with her strengths and sort out her other feelings when she could be alone.

Chapter Seven

The mechanic had assured Barrie that her truck would be finished by noon the next day, and she was going to keep him to that. While she didn't have any scheduled appointments, there was always the possibility of an emergency call. She needed her truck. Curtis had been kind to help her out yesterday, but she couldn't allow that to get out of hand. She was still attracted to him— frustrating as that was—and the memory of his hand on her back warmed her. They'd always had chemistry, and that had been the problem. She hadn't been thinking straight when she married Curtis; it had been a heady mix of passion and defiance that she'd lived to regret.

Earlier in the morning, Barrie's father had called her during his break at work. She always had been Daddy's girl, and even at the age of thirty-seven, she liked it when her father checked in.

"Just calling to make sure you're okay, sweetheart," he'd said. "And to see if you need me to talk to the mechanic for you."

"Dad, I can do that alone." She'd chuckled. "I'm not sixteen."

"If you need me, though—"

"Dad, I'll always need you," she'd reassured him. "But not for the mechanic today. I'll be fine."

He'd grudgingly let her go and headed back to work, but she appreciated the thought. Her dad made her feel safe in that elemental way that fathers had.

When noon approached, Barrie locked up her clinic and headed down the street toward the garage. The day was overcast and little shards of snow spun down from the sky. The temperature had dropped overnight and she wrapped her scarf a little closer around her neck.

Hope's downtown shops were decorated for Christmas, the lights in the windows glowing comfortingly into the snowy street. Their radiance was especially welcome since the low clouds kept the day darker than normal. Barrie walked past the drugstore's display window, which had a faux fireplace with stockings hung. Some wrapped boxes sat in the far corner beside a plate of half-eaten cookies. The bookstore had books wrapped in colorful paper stacked in the shape of a Christmas tree. The bakery next door had chocolate yule logs on display, as well as plates of elegantly decorated shortbread cookies, and she paused at that window, her heart filling with sadness.

Mom, I miss you so much...

Barrie had been trying her hand at shortbread cookies for weeks now—a connection to her mother that she just couldn't get right. They always ended up brittle and tasteless, and her cookie icing skills were amateur at best. Her fixation on recreating her mom's cookies had been taking over her free time. She knew that she couldn't replace her mom's presence in her life with a plate of perfectly turned out shortbread cookies, but she had such cozy memories associated with them that she wanted to be able to do the same for her own child. Then she could say, "My mom used to bake these, too," and Gwyneth wouldn't be quite so far away…

Barrie's veterinary practice was on the east end of Montana Avenue, and Hope Auto was on the west end, so her walk was a direct one—straight through downtown. Her toes were chilled through her boots by the time she reached the auto shop, and she pulled open the main door with a shiver.

No one was in the office. She let the door shut behind her, listening to the soft chime of the motion detector that let the mechanic know someone had come in. She shook the snow from her coat and waited for a few moments before the side door opened and Norm Reed came in, wiping his hands on an oil-stained cloth.

"Morning, Dr. Jones," Norm said. "You here to pick up your truck?"

"I am," she replied.

"I've got some bad news there," Norm said, and her stomach sank.

"Is the fix worse than you thought?" she asked.

"No, not that," he replied. "Brent's kid is sick, so he couldn't come in today. I'm on my own, and I haven't gotten to your truck yet."

"Oh…" She sighed. "Norm, I can't run my practice without my vehicle."

"I know, I know. And it's top priority. I'll have it

done by morning. That's a promise. I'll stay here all night if I have to. Is that fair enough?"

"It'll have to be," she said with a tired smile. "Thanks, Norm. I appreciate it."

Norm hooked a thumb toward the garage. "I'll get back to it, then. I'll call if it's done early."

Barrie exited the shop and started back down Montana Avenue. Everything seemed to be slipping lately, and that was part of her dedication to those blasted cookies. She was cautious by nature, and she didn't do anything without a proper plan in place—she'd done well following that rule. But this baby hadn't been planned, and neither had Curtis's arrival in town. She'd worked so hard to get her life safe and orderly, and Curtis had breezed in, determined to sell her building. So yes, she needed to feel in control of something that mattered, something she could pass on.

Barrie's stomach growled. She was always hungry lately, and she might as well stop at the Vanilla Bean for a Danish and a coffee. There wasn't much else she could do today. At the very least, she could enjoy a few minutes in Hope's only coffee shop.

When she got to the Vanilla Bean, she could smell the sweet scent of coffee from the sidewalk. Her stomach rumbled again, and she pulled open the door and stepped into the welcome warmth. The shop had a few patrons scattered inside, and as Barrie approached the counter to place her order, someone called her name.

She turned to see her good friend Mallory Cruise sitting by the window, her four-year-old son, Beau, opposite her. Barrie waved.

"I'm coming right over," she said. "Let me just order."

Mallory gave her a thumbs-up, and Barrie ordered a decaf mocha latte with a cherry Danish on the side. Then she crossed the room to Mallory's table.

"How are you doing?" Mallory asked, moving her purse from the chair next to her so that Barrie could sit.

"I'm fine," Barrie said. "How are you all?"

"Katie's in school," Beau, the four-year-old, announced. "And I'm having a treat without her."

Barrie got herself settled, her latte and Danish in front of her. "You're lucky, Beau."

"Yup," Beau agreed, biting into his chocolate muffin.

Mallory was married to Mike Cruise, one of the cops on the force here in Hope. She'd arrived in town only a few years ago, but she was already a solid part of the community. Barrie and Mallory had hit it off almost as soon as they met.

"We're all fine," Mallory said, answering her earlier question with a smile. "We're going to Disneyland next month."

"Are you really?" Barrie said, taking a sip of her latte. "When did this happen?"

"Mike surprised me for my birthday. Or he tried to…" Mallory chuckled. "The travel agent called our home to clarify which room we wanted yesterday."

Barrie laughed. "He tried."

"And I'm not complaining," Mallory said with a grin. "You're still coming to the Christmas party, aren't you?"

The party… Barrie grimaced. She'd completely forgotten. She wasn't in the mood to dress up and make nice—not with everything on her plate lately.

"I have nothing to wear," Barrie said. And that was the truth. "I have some jeans, and I've got a few big sweaters, but I'm in no way set up for a party, Mal."

"Let me take you shopping." Mallory's eyes lit up. "I never got to do that stuff, either. I was hiding the first half of my pregnancy and then I was on bedrest for the last half of it, so there were no cute maternity outfits for me."

"I don't know..." Barrie had never been into fashion, and shopping for new clothes had always been mildly intimidating.

"Trust me," Mallory said. "You'll feel better once you own something that fits properly. Let me take you shopping, and there's no pressure to buy."

"This is more for you than it is for me, isn't it?" Barrie asked with a small smile.

"Maybe." Mallory chuckled.

Barrie's phone rang, and she glanced down at the number. "Oh, it's Leanne from 4-H. I'd better take this."

Mallory nodded and turned her attention to Beau, who had slopped some hot chocolate onto the tabletop.

"Hi, Leanne," Barrie said. "How are you doing?"

"Not too badly," Leanne replied, but she sounded slightly nervous. "I needed to speak with you."

"Oh?" Barrie turned away from the table and ducked her head for a bit more privacy. "What's going on?"

"It's delicate," Leanne said, and there was apology in her tone. "First of all, I need you to know that this has nothing to do with me. When we voted, I voted for you, but a lot of the mothers have been raising concerns."

"About what, exactly?" Barrie asked, misgivings rising up inside her.

"About you speaking to the girls next week," Leanne said. "They're concerned that your pregnancy might be a distraction."

"From what?" Barrie couldn't help the flatness that entered her tone. "I'll be talking about veterinary care. I'm not doing a belly dance."

"They're young and impressionable," Leanne said. "And your pregnancy has been the talk of the town for weeks now."

"So I'm an unwed professional who happens to be pregnant, and that makes me a danger to their morals?" Barrie wasn't even trying to hide her irritation now. They'd asked *her* to talk to the girls, and she'd agreed. She hadn't gone looking for this.

"It's not me!" Leanne insisted.

"Is it Jen Hartfield?" Barrie asked with a sigh. For all of her compassion for Jen's history, she was getting really tired of being the target around here.

"Not only her," Leanne said. "I got outvoted. I don't think it should be an issue, but the other mothers do. They think you're a bad example."

Barrie had put herself through veterinary school, had set up her own practice and was serious competition to the only other vet in town. But her pregnancy seemed to be more important to these women than her professional accomplishments.

"So you're canceling," Barrie clarified.

"I'm afraid so."

"Thanks for the call," Barrie said curtly.

"No hard feelings, Dr. Jones," Leanne said. "We wish it could have worked out."

"Of course. Take care." Barrie hung up, and her cheeks burned. When she turned back toward the table, she found Mallory's eyes pinned to her.

Mallory winced. "Is that what it sounded like?"

"Probably." Barrie pulled a hand through her hair. "Leanne says I'm a bad influence on the girls, and they're canceling my talk."

"That's downright insulting." Mallory shook her head. "What is this, 1950?"

Mallory had been pregnant when she'd arrived in Hope. Her boyfriend had left her for her best friend, and when he discovered Mal was pregnant, he offered to pay for the abortion. That baby was now sitting across from them, slurping hot chocolate. Mallory was now married, but some of the bigger prudes in this town hadn't forgotten.

"How bad are the rumors about me?" Barrie asked.

"You don't want to hear about that," Mallory replied. "It's just stupid talk."

"I do," Barrie pressed. "I mean, if I'm getting treated like the scarlet woman around here, I should probably know why. What are they saying?"

"People's imaginations are far worse than reality," Mallory said. "Most of the time. They make up the worst stories possible."

"Like what?" Barrie asked.

"Like you're pregnant with a married man's child," Mal

replied with a sigh. "And they've been finger-pointing at a few candidates around town…"

"Oh, for crying out loud!" Barrie shook her head. They were right, ironically enough, but the married man wasn't from Hope, and she'd had no idea he was married to begin with. But Leanne's husband had cheated on her twice in the last five years, so maybe Leanne wasn't quite so supportive of Barrie as she claimed, if there were stories circulating that Barrie was a home-wrecker. No hard feelings, indeed.

"Why don't you just tell the truth about the father of the baby?" Mallory asked quietly. "I'm sure it can't be as bad as people imagine. It'll stop the tongue wagging, at least."

"No." Barrie turned her latte slowly in front of her. If she kept quiet, at least she'd have deniability. And some semblance of privacy. Her mistake at the veterinary convention was humiliating enough without offering it up for public chatter.

"I'm here if you want to vent," Mallory said. "And you can trust my discretion."

"Thanks, but I'm not ready to do that." Barrie didn't feel the need to vent; she needed to solve her own problems and set up her life so that she could raise her child on her own. Besides, as soon as she told one person, the story would get out. It might be overheard, or a text might be seen. Someone might see Mallory's face when they suggested some theory… The possibilities were endless. A secret was no longer a secret once she told the first person.

"Okay." Mallory didn't look offended, to Barrie's relief. "But I'm here for you, Barrie. You know that."

Barrie reached over and squeezed her friend's hand. "Absolutely."

"Miss Barrie?" Beau said quietly.

"Yes, Beau?" Barrie turned her attention to the boy.

"Are you going to eat that?" He pointed at her Danish.

"Beau!" Mallory chided. "That's rude. Don't ask people for food. Good grief!"

"It's okay," Barrie said with a low laugh. "I'm going to eat most of it, but I'll give you a piece, okay?"

Beau seemed pleased with this option, and she tore him off a chunk of pastry. Right now, Barrie might not have a husband, the conception of her child might be her biggest embarrassment so far and she had no idea how she was going to balance everything once this baby arrived, but she'd heard somewhere that all a person could do was take the next right step. She'd try that, because she couldn't see the bigger solutions for the life of her.

CURTIS LOADED BAGS of dog food, salt licks for the cattle and several bags of ear tags into the back of his truck in the parking lot of Hope Ranch and Supply. His mind had been on Barrie all morning, no matter how hard he tried to distract himself with work. It wasn't just memories from their marriage that had left him uncomfortably preoccupied. It was her as a mature woman, and not just her pregnancy like she'd suggested. She was the kind of woman who'd grown more beautiful as the years went by—and more interesting. He liked having an excuse to be around her, and he knew he was playing with emotional fire here. It had taken him years to get over her, and falling for her again would be a terrible idea.

His cell phone rang just as he slammed the tailgate shut, and he rooted out his phone with a sigh. He glanced down at the number.

"Betty?" he said, picking up.

"Curtis, I'm at the barn, and there's another sick cow," his aunt said. "I don't have Barrie's number in my phone, only Dr. Berton's, but Barrie has been dealing with this outbreak, so I think we'd better stick with her for the time being. Can you give her a call and get her to come by?"

Curtis had Barrie's business card in his wallet, so contacting his ex-wife wouldn't be an issue. "Aunty, what are you doing in the barn?"

"If you hadn't noticed, this is still my ranch!" she quipped. "Now quit trying to babysit me and give the vet a call, would you?"

"Sure thing," he said. "Don't break anything new."

"Har har," his aunt replied, and hung up without a farewell.

Curtis smiled wryly, then pulled out the business card. Betty might have asked him to help out, but holding her back from running her ranch wasn't even a possibility. He paused before he dialed Barrie's number.

He was actually looking forward to calling her, and he recognized the problem there... He was starting to get attached again, and he needed to stop this. He was leaving town, and her life didn't include him. If only his feelings could catch up with his brain.

"Dr. Jones," she intoned as she picked up.

"Hi, Barrie, it's Curtis." He cleared his throat.

"Oh…hi. Everything okay?"

"Betty just let me know that there's another sick cow. They have it in the barn, but she needs you to come down. Are you free?"

"My truck is still in the shop," she replied. "I'm sorry about that. You might want to—"

Call Palmer Berton… Yeah, he could, but he didn't want to.

"Where are you?" he interrupted.

"Downtown. The Vanilla Bean," she replied.

"Great. I'm at the Ranch and Supply. I could pick you up, if you want. You're the one who's been dealing with this outbreak, so you're our go-to for this."

"And I'm happy to do it," she said.

"Would you be ready in ten minutes?"

"Not a problem," she replied.

"See you soon."

Curtis hung up and hopped into the cab of his truck. He could still make out the soft scent of her perfume in the vehicle from yesterday. It was the same scent she used to wear when they were married, and a long-forgotten memory surfaced of her standing in front of their dresser in a pink summer dress, spritzing some perfume onto her wrists… But somehow in that memory, he aged her into the woman she was now.

He started the truck and pulled out of the parking space. The Ranch and Supply was located on the west end of town along the highway, but Hope being as small as it was, he was only five minutes away from downtown and the coffee shop. When he turned onto Main, he could already see Barrie standing on the street, waiting for him. The wind blew her straight hair, and she hunched her shoulders. He wasn't going to get used to seeing her pregnant. She was right. Her condition certainly did soften him toward her, but it wasn't just a testosterone reaction to a pregnant woman. She was vulnerable, and whatever it was that set Barrie Jones off balance sparked a protective instinct inside him. It just so happened to be a pregnancy.

Curtis pulled up to the curb, and Barrie crossed the street. He leaned across the cab to open the door for her, and she climbed inside.

"We'll need to stop by my clinic for my bag," she said as she fastened her seat belt.

"Hi," he said, and her cheeks colored.

"Sorry, hi."

Curtis signaled, pulled a U-turn and headed back down Montana Avenue toward her clinic. The last time he'd been there, she'd told him to back out of her life, and it was like she'd put up an emotional fence around that place. It had worked—he didn't feel welcome anymore.

Curtis glanced over at her, and Barrie's expression was grim.

"You okay?" he asked.

"Huh?" She forced a smile. "I'm fine. So, tell me about the cow."

Was it him making her so uncomfortable? Or was there something else?

"The same as the others, I'm assuming," he said.

"Betty just called and asked me to get you, so I haven't seen it myself... But you're not fine."

She licked her lips, then sighed. "I'll figure it out. It's not that big of a deal."

"Is it me?" he asked. "Have I crossed a line, or ticked you off?"

"Not everything is about you, Curtis." She gave him a smile.

"Good. I'm glad it's not me," he said. "So, what is it?"

They were approaching her clinic, and he slowed and put on his turn signal. Another pickup passed in the other direction, and Curtis waited until the road was clear before making the turn.

"It's just gossip around town," she said as he pulled into the parking lot in front of her clinic and chose the spot near her door.

"So, what's fueling the gossip this time?" He put the truck into Park and turned toward her.

"They're trying to guess at the father of my baby."

Curtis eyed her, watching for her reaction. She looked away. "That's kind of insulting, but not surprising, right?" he said. "You've got to ignore them."

"And I was," she replied, pushing the door open and letting in a rush of cold air. "But now my talk with the 4-H girls has been canceled because of it."

Barrie eased herself down and slammed the door behind her. He watched her head to the clinic and unlock the door. She disappeared inside while her words spun through his mind. He remembered Hope's tenacious gossip, but could it really have gone so far? That pissed him off. Barrie deserved better from this town.

A couple of minutes later, Barrie emerged with her black bag in hand. Curtis leaned over and pushed the door open from the inside, then grabbed the bag to give her room to get in. Once she was settled, he headed for the highway.

"What happened?" he asked.

"Leanne Perkins called a few minutes ago and let me know that my pregnancy was a distraction, and they worried for the impressionable girls."

"Girls who've all seen cows inseminated and calves born," he retorted.

"I'm a scandal."

He caught the quiver in her voice. This was no joke to her—this had hurt her, and he felt a rise in that old protectiveness.

"You're a professional and a good person," he shot back. "Leanne Perkins is an idiot. Wait…is this because of Jen Hartfield?"

"Leanne insists that it wasn't only her," Barrie said. "The mothers voted."

Curtis sighed. There had been a time when Hope had turned on him—but he'd had the luxury of leaving. Still, he knew what it felt like to have an entire town make up its mind about him.

"How much does this presentation matter to you?" he asked.

"I cared about it," she said. "I want to encourage girls to work in agriculture. We need women in this field, and if I can encourage just one girl to become a vet—"

"They'll be encouraged by you simply being a vet," he said. "You show them that it's possible. Like the Hartfield girl."

Barrie was silent for a moment, and then she said, "I'm not used to being the cautionary tale, Curtis."

He slowed at the intersection and signaled a turn onto the highway. It was a straight drive out to the Porter ranch from here, and he settled back into his seat. The telephone lines looped past the truck window, and he glanced at the fences sagging in snow drifts. The clouds hung low, threatening more snow.

"You might consider stopping the gossip by just telling people who the father is," he said after a moment.

"You aren't the only one to suggest that, but it isn't their business," she replied. "This is my body, my baby, my mistake!"

"No child is a mistake," he said. "Not every family starts the same way. My mom was a teenager when she had me, and we still count as a family."

"I'm not calling my *baby* a mistake," she said, tears misting her eyes. "But I messed up. I'm not the kind of woman who goes around having one-night stands. I know that consequences matter and that they can dog you for a lifetime. I was the responsible girl who studied hard. Even after you, I made sure that my choices were solid so I could have a bright future. I'm not the irresponsible sort!"

"I know." Did he ever know. She'd been cautious and proper from the start, and that had been part of her allure. He liked the idea of teaching her a little bit of fun.

"Do you? Because apparently, the entire town now

questions that." She shook her head. "I'm a professional. I work hard. I got myself through school, and I built something for myself. That should count."

"So it was a one-night stand?" he asked.

She'd said more than she'd planned, he could tell. She shot him a cautious look. "It doesn't matter."

"You're right," he said. "It doesn't. What you do romantically isn't anyone else's business."

"Thank you."

And yet he still wanted to get his hands on whatever moron had done this to her... But who was he to get on a high horse? He'd walked out on her, too. Had she been shaken—like this? But she'd kicked him out. He never would have left her otherwise. He just hadn't fit into her responsibly planned life anymore.

"If you ask me, you were always too careful," he said.

"Since when?" she asked, irritation in her voice.

"Since always," he said. "The biggest risk you took was marrying me, and then you shut down. You wouldn't risk anything, and maybe it's time you did."

"I'm thirty-seven," she said. "I have what...twenty-five years left to work? I have to pay off my house. I have to get ready for retirement—"

"You've got twenty-eight years left to work," he retorted, "and you're having a baby. You always liked to plan everything, and this wasn't planned. Well, the best things are a surprise. I say, enjoy it. Quit beating yourself up, and ignore the people who are going to judge you, because I have news for you, Barrie—if they're judging you now, they were doing it before, just a little more quietly."

"You think?" she asked.

"I'm pretty certain," he replied.

The highway was plowed clean, but some spots on the asphalt shone wet. Seeing as the temperature was well below freezing, it was ice. He let up on the gas and slowed down a little. He had a pregnant woman with him in the truck, after all.

"Curtis, how do you do it?" she asked. "I mean, how do you just see what happens, and not worry?"

"I have faith in my own abilities," he said. "I'm relatively certain that I can handle whatever comes."

She sighed. "I don't bounce back as well as you do."

"You think I did?"

"You're the one who left," she replied. "I'm assuming you did."

He sighed. "I left because I was constantly disappointing you. You married me because you loved me, but you expected things I couldn't deliver."

"I didn't."

"Sure you did. Like money," he replied. "You knew I was a bull rider when we got married. That was no surprise, but once we said our vows, the things you used to accept about me were no longer okay with you. You wanted a certain income, a certain life, and you had an image of what you wanted me to become, but you never stopped to ask if I wanted to be that guy."

"I wanted you to be my husband!" Barrie shook her head.

"Yeah, but you seemed to think that me following my dreams meant I wasn't committed."

"It wasn't that," she said.

"No? Then what was it?"

Barrie sighed. "I had dreams, too. You didn't seem willing to compromise. When I told you to leave, I was just so tired. I was tired of fighting and being hurt and wondering what you were thinking or feeling. I was just so tired of it all."

"And I can understand that," he said. "Now, at least. But do you know what it's like to look into your wife's eyes and see disappointment, maybe even a little regret?"

Barrie was silent.

"It hurts. A lot. When I married you, I wanted to give you everything. But I was only good at one thing, and that was bull riding. I'd made promises to you about how I'd provide, and then you didn't want me to use my one skill to do that."

"There were stable jobs—" she started.

"There were, but I was…me." He cast her a sad smile. "I wasn't cut out for that stuff, Barrie. I'm a bit of a lone wolf in a lot of ways. If you'd married some other guy, he'd have been able to give you all the stuff I couldn't afford yet, and I knew that. I wanted to give you all of that, but… I had to do it my own way."

"You sound like I wanted a certain lifestyle," she said. "I wasn't expecting money, Curtis. I wanted time with you. I wanted some regularity, something I could count on."

"You could count on my love," he said gruffly.

"Until you left." Her voice was low, but the words stabbed.

He'd left, and he'd never live that one down, would

he? Curtis sighed. "Yeah. I left, but you no longer wanted what I had to offer. Everyone has their limits, I guess. I couldn't change who I was, and you wouldn't be happy with what I could give. There didn't seem to be any way to fix that."

She was silent.

"You said I bounced back, but I didn't," he went on. "I'd given you everything I could—all I had—and it wasn't enough. That gutted me. So I looked in your eyes, and I saw the way you looked at me—the way you saw me… You saw a loser, someone lower than you, someone you couldn't respect. I didn't bounce back from that. Ever."

"I didn't think you were a loser," she said quietly.

"Did you trust me to provide for you?" he asked. "Did you trust me to take care of you, or did you think you needed to fix me first?"

She didn't answer, and he glanced over at her. Her expression was somber.

"Don't worry about it," he said. "I didn't mean to say all that, anyway. I just wanted you to know that I didn't waltz off and forget you. I crawled off and licked my wounds for a really long time. If that helps at all."

He was supposed to come to town and take care of his business with as little fuss as possible. This— whatever he and Barrie were doing—hadn't been part of the plan.

"It does help a little bit," she said after a few beats of silence.

He wasn't sure how he felt about that, but whatever. He wasn't supposed to be getting attached. He'd have to be more careful—and put a lid on whatever he was feeling. He hadn't been enough for her when he was an able-bodied bull rider, and he wouldn't be enough for her now. He'd do well to remember that.

Chapter Eight

When Barrie arrived at the barn, another two heifers were ill besides the one Curtis knew about. Barrie's work was cut out for her. One of the original calves had taken a turn for the worse, and Barrie set the calf up with more heat and an extra shot of antibiotics. One of the goat's kids wasn't getting enough milk, so they bottle-fed the little thing. By the time Barrie had finished in the Porter barn, the sun had set and her whole body ached.

She'd been thinking about Curtis's words in the truck that morning. She'd never realized what he'd been feeling back then, but it was still hard to pity him. He'd left, and that had ended everything. He could have talked to her—actually put those feelings out there! He could have explained his position. They could have gone for couple's counseling. Anything! Walking away wasn't the only option. She hadn't backed him into a corner, and in her defense, she'd had something to offer to their relationship, too, if he'd only stopped to look. Their marriage wasn't about him taking care of her. It was about two people loving each other and going after their dreams. Both of them. Not just him.

But his question had been plaguing her: had she trusted him to take care of her? If she had to be utterly honest, the answer was no. She hadn't. She'd wanted to stay in Hope because while she loved Curtis, she needed the security of her home and family close by. He'd been right—she'd wanted more than he was offering, and she was afraid to take her eyes off the shore.

Barrie followed Curtis out of the barn into evening twilight. A sliver of a moon hung low, and the strongest of the stars were but pinpricks on the gray velvet of the sky. In the west, the horizon still glowed red.

Her feet and back ached, and Barrie felt like her body was betraying her. If this was how her body handled a pregnancy at five months, what was it going to be like at eight or nine? She put a hand into the small of her back and straightened.

"You okay?" Curtis tossed a plastic bag of salt blocks into the back of his pickup truck.

"Fine."

"Yeah, you don't look fine," he said. "Come on, I'll drive you home. Thanks for all of this today."

"It's my job," she said.

"And I'm still grateful." He arched an eyebrow.

Barrie smiled, then shook her head. "You're welcome."

Curtis pulled open the passenger side door, then headed around to the driver's side. Apparently he'd learned not to offer any more hands up, but she secretly appreciated the gesture of the opened door. The baby moved inside her as she hoisted herself up into the cab with a sigh. She slammed the door shut and stretched her legs out, giving her feet a much-needed rest.

"Can I get you a burger or something?" he asked.

She was hungry—there was no denying that—but her body was sore and all she wanted was to get back to the house. She wanted to sink into her couch, put her feet up and eat something microwaveable.

"I'm exhausted," she said. "But thanks anyway. Besides, Miley has been home alone all day."

"No problem. Straight home, then."

Curtis put the truck into gear and pulled away from the barn. The headlights sliced through the darkness, but Barrie's attention wasn't on the road ahead of them—it was on the fields out her window. Moonlight sparkled over the cold-hardened snow, and there was something so peaceful in the scene that she could feel the tension seep out of her shoulders and back.

"So, what are your plans for Christmas?" Curtis asked.

Barrie glanced toward him, but Curtis's eyes were on the road ahead, and he changed gears as they drove past Betty's house and headed toward the main road.

"What I always do," she said. "Dinner with my parents. Well, I guess just Dad this year."

"That's it?" He shot her a quick look. "You were always more into Christmas than that."

"It was different then," she replied. "I was married."

Curtis chewed on the side of his cheek, and she inwardly winced. She was tired and achy and apparently her filter wasn't working as it should. She remembered all the love she'd poured into their two Christmases together. From the cooking to the decorating, she'd done everything she could to make their home glow for him.

"You did make a nice Christmas, Barrie," he said.

For all the good it had done… "Do you have any idea how hard I worked at our marriage?" she asked, adjusting herself in her seat so she could see him better. "I poured everything I had into making our home warm and special." She shook her head, unsure of how to encapsulate it all in words.

"There was nothing wrong with our home," he said.

"Nothing wrong with it…" Tears misted her eyes, and it was the exhaustion, she knew, because this pain was so old that it shouldn't logically matter. "Curtis, I was aiming for something a little better than that."

"You know what I mean." He sighed.

"No, I don't!" She pulled a hand through her hair. "I did everything I knew to make our home into a place where you'd feel…at home! I planted the garden, I canned fruit, I made those orange peel scents for our drawers, I—" She stopped, feeling exhausted even remembering it all. "I did that for you, and you never seemed to notice. And I was the idiot who never saw that you'd have one foot out the door no matter what I did."

"I noticed." He shook his head. "I just didn't care about those things like you did. I thought you were doing it for you."

"Like Christmas," she confirmed bitterly.

"Yeah, like Christmas! I don't know. I never really did too much for Christmas at home with Mom. She usually had a gig over the holidays, and I could go watch her sing, or I could stay home and watch TV. I mean… Whatever. It wasn't that big of a deal."

"Christmas is *always* a big deal," she retorted. It was supposed to be, at least. Traditions held a family together.

"Not to you. At least, not anymore," he shot back. "You're having dinner with your dad as usual, I thought."

She didn't like having her own words tossed back at her, especially by the man who had no right to even ask about her personal plans.

"Well, it's different now," she replied. "When I had you, I had someone to create some traditions for. I wanted to make a home for you that would always call you back…" Emotion tightened her throat, and she stopped talking.

"There was nothing wrong with our home," he repeated, and she heard sadness in his voice. "But you were so stuck in it. It was just an old house with some used furniture. And you made the most of it—don't get me wrong—but it wasn't about that for me. It never was."

Barrie swallowed hard and leaned her head back. "I know. It's okay. It doesn't matter."

"No, let me say my piece," he countered. "You keep saying that you poured yourself into making a home for us, and I know you did. I saw how hard you worked on it. But I didn't want a home like that. I wanted a woman by my side."

"And where was that woman supposed to live?" She almost laughed at the ridiculousness of it all.

"With me," he said. "Wherever we happened to be."

"In some ratty trailer," she said. "Or a tent. Or a one-star hotel."

"We were young and in love. What did it matter?" He shot her a small smile—that tempting kind of smile that made her stomach flip. But that had been his way—cajole her into some adventure, and then see what happened.

"It mattered," she replied. "I needed more security than that."

Following her bull riding husband around the circuit wasn't the kind of life she needed. She had plans for her own education, but more than that, she needed money in the bank and a roof over her head. She wasn't the kind of woman who liked uncertainty.

"I know." He sighed. "Matching sheets, scented drawers…that iron skillet your parents got us for a wedding present. You needed that stuff to feel like you were safe. Thing is, Barrie, I wanted you to need *me* to feel safe."

"It wasn't just about our home," she said. "I had dreams and ambitions, too, and I couldn't pursue those if I was trailing along with you on the circuit. On top of which, what is this—the 1950s? It wasn't just about provision. It was about making a life together, and you were really bad at compromise."

"I wasn't against you becoming a vet," he said.

"You just weren't willing to make room for it," she replied.

"And we come full circle again," he said. "We wanted really different things out of life, and we didn't talk about that soon enough."

They fell into silence, and snow began to fall in lazy flakes, blurring their vision through the windshield. They were approaching town, and Curtis slowed as he came to the turnoff.

"Barrie, you did well for yourself," he said as he took the turn. "You've put together a great life here in Hope, and you should be proud. Looking at the results, you made the right choice."

"What choice?" she asked. "Staying in town? Going to school?"

"Kicking me out." He met her gaze for only a moment, but she read sadness in those dark eyes.

"Like I said before," she replied, "I might have kicked you out, but you *left*."

"Yeah. I did." He signaled the last turn onto her road, and she felt a wave of sadness of her own. She hadn't actually wanted to win that one. She didn't know what she'd hoped he'd say...or maybe she did. She wished that just once she could hear Curtis Porter tell her that the life she'd offered him had been the best option all along. But he wasn't going to say that, because even now, fifteen years after the fact, the home she'd poured her heart into creating still wasn't enough to tempt him.

CURTIS PULLED INTO Barrie's drive and leaned back in the seat. He wasn't sure what she was feeling right now, but he knew that bringing up the past had been a bad idea. This was all fifteen years ago, and he was leaving town just as soon as Christmas was over... What use was there in dredging up old hurts? They'd made the choice back then and gotten divorced. It was over.

The snow was coming steadily down now. He turned off the engine, and they fell into that velvety silence. She looked pale in the moonlight—paler than usual.

"Barrie, are you alright?" he asked.

"I'm tired," she said quietly. "And sore."

"You should have said earlier." He unfastened his seat belt. "Come on. Let's get you in."

"I'm fine—"

"Yeah?" He wasn't taking that answer this time. "Well, so am I. And I'm getting you all the way inside." He pushed open his door and hopped out. When he got around to her side, she was just sliding down to the ground, wincing as her feet hit the concrete.

Curtis slammed the door shut for her and took her arm in his. She didn't argue this time, which told him she wasn't alright. He knew nothing about pregnancies—but he knew Barrie, and she'd been putting on a brave face for longer than she should have. He was willing to bet on it.

When they approached the door, the scramble of toenails and a joyous woof greeted them from the other side.

"Miley missed me," she said, pulling out her key.

Curtis followed her in, and after Miley licked his mistress, the dog turned his attention to Curtis.

"Hey, there," Curtis said, holding out his hand. Miley bounced up and planted both paws on Curtis's shoulders. He was a big dog, and about as heavy as a weaned calf, too. He stuck his wet nose into Curtis's face.

"Miley!" Barrie chastised him. "Get down!"

Miley did as he was told, and turned a few circles around the linoleum.

Curtis looked around the kitchen. "Barrie, go sit down. I'll get you some supper."

"Curtis, no—"

"Take this as my apology for being terrible at compromise back in the day," he said. "You're right—I was pretty focused on my own career and didn't bother to see what you really wanted. Well, today you overdid it on my watch. I'm making you something to eat."

Barrie looked ready to argue. Then she glanced at the couch and her expression softened. He'd just won this one. Sort of. She walked toward the couch, her movements slow and cautious. Then she sank down onto the seat and heaved a sigh. As Curtis took off his boots and hat, Miley hopped up onto the couch, too, then settled his massive self onto what was left of Barrie's lap.

"Isn't he heavy?" Curtis asked.

"Like you wouldn't believe." She chuckled. "But he missed me."

"Miley, you want to go out to pee?" Curtis called. He spotted a bag of dog food on the counter, and he grabbed what he assumed was a dog bowl on the floor—except it was more the size of a mixing bowl. He filled it and put in onto the floor. The dog leaped down from Barrie's lap and beelined for the door. Curtis opened it, and Miley headed for the snow and lifted a leg.

"Thanks." She leaned her head back. "And I hate to

point this out, but I don't remember you knowing how to cook anything more than toast."

"And I made the perfect toast, too," he said with a low laugh. "But you haven't seen me in a good long while, Barrie. Some things have changed."

Miley came back in and headed for his food bowl. Meanwhile, Curtis poked through her cupboards and then her fridge. He came up with some sausage, a tomato, a few eggs and a loaf of bread. He was good for that toast. In his rummaging, he came across a tin of cookies. Curious, he opened it and found some shards of what were probably meant to be shortbread cookies.

"What happened here?" he asked, shaking the tin.

"Oh, don't ask. I can't get them right," she said.

"I've gotten pretty good at cookies recently," he said.

"What?" She opened her eyes and fixed him with a curious stare. "Since when?"

"I took a class." He met her gaze, then felt the heat rising in his face. "To impress a woman."

"Was she impressed?" Barrie raised one eyebrow.

"She was." He chuckled. "It didn't work out, though."

"I'm trying to figure them out. It seems like a motherly thing to do, doesn't it? Mom made amazing shortbread cookies, and I just don't have the knack yet."

Gwyneth Jones had been a real artist when it came to baking, and he remembered Barrie trying her hand at her mother's cookies… No one could match Gwyneth, though. He set about chopping sausage, onion and some green pepper and tossed them into a pan. As he worked, he glanced again into the tin. They really hadn't turned out. He looked around the kitchen and spotted a wad of yarn behind the fruit bowl. When he pulled it out, he discovered what seemed to be the beginning of some knitting that also wasn't turning out. She was more than trying to get ready for this baby…and she was hitting a wall.

"So, you knit now, too?" he called over the sizzle of frying.

"No, I don't," she called back. "I'm terrible at it."

"What were you trying to make?" he asked.

"Booties. Not that you can tell."

Barrie, who'd longed to make a home for him, was attempting to do the same thing for this baby, and the realization stung. This wasn't just some attempt at a craft. She wouldn't have a whole lot of free time to fill that way. This was her effort to create a home that would…how had she said it? A home that would call her child back again. And she was failing—at least in the ways she was trying to make it work.

Barrie's eyes had closed, and she absently rubbed a hand over the dome of her stomach.

Looking at that little bundle of yarn, and at the shards of cookies in the tin, he wondered how much he had hurt her by not settling into that nest she'd so lovingly prepared for them. Would it have killed him to compliment the matching towels? It just hadn't seemed to matter back then, and he'd cared more about tugging her away from it all. But the more he coaxed, the deeper she dug in.

When the food was finished, he brought two plates out to the living room and handed her one.

"Thank you." She accepted a fork and immediately

set into the meal. He watched as she took a bite, then shot him a look of surprise. "This is really good!"

"You aren't the only one who grew up," he said. "I've improved. What can I say?"

She nodded and took another bite. He sank into the seat next to her, and they ate in silence for a couple of minutes, Barrie making little sounds of enjoyment as she chewed.

"You're going to be fine," he said.

She looked over at him, then swallowed. "It's what I keep saying."

"Yeah, but *I'm* telling you," he said. "You're going to be just fine. And you don't have to make shortbread or knit booties, or whatever else you've decided would make you the perfect mom."

"I'm not giving up on the cookies yet," she said, taking another bite.

"No?" He shrugged. "Thing is, kids like cookies, but they don't really care if you whip them up by hand or pass them a box from the grocery store."

"I care." Her voice was low, but he caught the depth of feeling in those words. This wasn't only about her child. This was about her needs, too. Maybe Barrie needed these trappings just as much as she thought everyone else did.

"Your kid will love you for what you are, Barrie," he said. "My mom made really good toast. She might not have been perfect, but man, I loved her."

Barrie's cheeks flushed and she met his gaze for a moment, then smiled. "Then I guess I have hope."

Barrie speared the last piece of sausage and popped

it into her mouth. He took her plate, put it on top of his and set them on the floor. Miley came over and licked every inch his tongue could touch, forks rattling against glass as he gave them his full attention.

"Give me your feet," Curtis said.

"What?" She looked honestly alarmed, and he grinned.

"Give me your feet, Barrie." He bent and lifted them into his lap as she pivoted on the sofa so she could lean back against the arm. He took one foot in his hands and started gently rubbing in slow, firm circles.

"You don't have to—"

"I know. Shut up already." He met her gaze, but he didn't stop working her feet with slow, measured strokes. He was defying her—daring her to turn this down. For a moment, she was tense, and he thought she might pull away, but then she sighed and shut her eyes.

"This is wildly inappropriate," she murmured.

"Probably," he agreed. "But it feels good."

"Hmm…"

With her eyes closed, he could let his gaze wander over the chestnut locks that framed her face, the roundness of her figure and her belly, down to her feet, which lay warm in his hands. He rubbed the arches of her feet, moving down to her toes—they were cute toes. He knew that from before. He could see her body relax, and he had to admit that he wasn't just thinking about being helpful right now…he was thinking about taking this a whole lot further.

He wouldn't. Obviously he wouldn't, but even pregnant and fifteen years older, she still drew him in. He could see the lines around her eyes, and how her lips were fuller with the pregnancy, or perhaps with her age. She was no longer a lithe twentysomething sweetheart. She was a mature woman with the full bust and plump thighs that made him long to slide his hands up them...

But he *wouldn't*. He swallowed. He wasn't the womanizing type. He'd rarely taken advantage of the offers he'd gotten from girls wanting to have a good time with him. But having Barrie lying on her couch with her feet in his hands...how on earth had this just become the sexiest thing he could imagine?

He kept massaging, watching her chest rise and fall in a slower and slower rhythm.

"Barrie," he murmured.

"I'm not asleep," she whispered, as if reading his mind, and her eyes fluttered open. She pushed herself up into a seated position, pulling her feet from his lap, and he regretted having disturbed the moment.

"Okay, well—" He swallowed, because his mind had been going along some dangerous paths there, and he had too many reasons not to mess with Barrie's peace of mind again. He needed to get out of here now before he did something he regretted.

"I'd better get going," he said. "I have an early morning."

She nodded. "Me, too."

"Look, about what we were discussing in the truck—"

"It was a long time ago, Curtis," she said with a faint shrug. "We were both a whole lot younger."

"Even if we hadn't lasted," Curtis said quietly, "I wish I'd done better by you."

"Yeah?" He watched as her lips formed the word, and she was so tempting... She always had been his weak spot.

"Yeah." She was close enough that he could have moved in and caught those lips with his, but instead, he sucked in a breath and pushed himself to his feet. "I'd better head out, Barrie."

"Okay. Thanks for dinner and the foot rub."

Curtis cast her a grin and headed toward the side door, where his boots and hat waited. He knew the limits of what he could endure, and he'd better get out of here before he took some serious advantage. Barrie followed him, Miley padding along behind her, and when he'd done up his coat and dropped his hat back on his head, he turned toward Barrie and found her closer than he'd thought. Her tired eyes widened in surprise, too, but before she could step back, he slid an arm around her waist and tugged her closer against him.

Her belly pressed against his abs, and he looked down at those plump, soft lips, feeling an undeniable hunger rise up inside him. He sucked in a breath. He shouldn't do it—he knew that. He should walk out and not give himself more to apologize for tomorrow. Barrie was pregnant, sexy as anything, but also vulnerable. This wasn't a game—

She rose onto the tips of her toes, and her eyes fluttered shut as her lips touched his so lightly that it almost tickled.

"Ah, hell..." he murmured, and he lowered his mouth

over hers, deepening the kiss, pulling her harder against him. The room evaporated around him, and there was only Barrie in his arms and her lips moving against his…

But then Miley gave a yip, and Barrie pulled back. Her cheeks blushed crimson and she touched her fingers to her mouth.

"I should go," he murmured.

She nodded. "Yes. Leave. Bye."

Curtis chuckled. Did she mean that? He doubted it. If he pressed the issue he could probably get her into his arms again…but this wasn't right.

"Okay," he said, pulling open the door. "I'll see you."

Barrie nodded, but her eyes still sparkled with that kiss. She'd felt it, too. He could tell. He stepped outside, and she shut the door firmly behind him. They had no business doing this again—it couldn't end well. But at least that kiss hadn't been one-sided. She'd felt it, too.

Chapter Nine

Barrie leaned against the door, shut her eyes and let out a soft moan. What had she just done? She'd started that, and he'd most definitely finished it. Kissing him had *not* been part of the plan!

Maybe it was his consideration in cooking for her and rubbing her feet... That had been the first time since she'd announced her pregnancy that anyone had done something like that for her. She didn't have a boyfriend, and she'd been so determined to prove she didn't need one that she hadn't been prepared for how good it would feel to have someone take care of her for a change. Add to that his way of looking at her, which had always dissolved her reserve...

"What was I thinking?" She opened her eyes and found Miley staring at her with a look of reproach on his canine face. "I know. It was a bad idea."

And if only that kiss had proved he couldn't still make her feel like she was floating...if only that part had changed. But it hadn't...or more accurately, their level of attraction hadn't changed, but kissing him *had* been different than before... Curtis was no longer the eager twenty-year-old. He was a man who had showed some reserve, some self-control. And when he'd finally kissed her, there was something deeper, more urgent than she'd ever sensed from him.

She didn't get to blame this one on him, either. That was irritating, too. He'd been holding himself back. Sure, he'd pulled her close, but she'd seen the battle on his face, and she'd made the choice for him.

"Stupid, stupid, stupid," she muttered to herself as she flicked the lock on the door and headed toward her bedroom. Was she really so vulnerable right now that a little bit of kindness and a foot rub could empty her head of all logical thought? Curtis was still the same guy he always was. He'd only just stopped bull riding, and it had taken him fifteen years to give it up! This wasn't a different man, just an older version of the same guy who'd never been husband enough.

Barrie sank onto the side of her bed. She had a baby coming, and enough problems of her own that the last thing she needed was more complication... She wouldn't do that again.

Her cell phone rang, and Barrie looked at the number. She heaved a sigh, then picked up the call.

"Dr. Berton?" she said.

"Dr. Jones. How are you doing?"

"Fine, thanks," she replied. "What can I do for you?"

There was a pause. "Can I call you Barrie?"

"If I can call you Palmer." She was in no mood to be patronized today.

"Fair enough," he replied. "Barrie, I have a proposition for you."

"Oh?" She didn't even try to hide the wariness in her tone.

"I want you to work for me again," he said.

"You've got to be joking," she retorted. "We've done this before, Palmer. We don't work well together. I drive you crazy, if you'll recall."

"You're a good vet."

"I'm more than good," she said. "I'm also rather stubborn and do things my own way."

"I'd pay you well, provide health insurance and give you a more regular schedule. With the baby coming, I'm sure that would be helpful."

"Where is this coming from?" she asked.

"I think it would be beneficial for both of us," he replied. "I'm getting older, and I find it hard to keep up with the caseload. But still, I have the most clients, and I have thirty years of experience in this community. You're having a baby soon, and you won't be able to keep up with the emergency calls anymore. We could both benefit from working together."

"Under your shingle," she clarified.

"Yes. I've worked for this longer. I'm sure you can recognize that."

"I've worked for this, too," she said.

"Be reasonable…" Palmer sighed.

"I'm not interested." She covered her eyes with one hand. "I'm sorry."

"Barrie, I'm a father. I know the changes in your life that are coming up. Babies take over everything—"

"I've worked too hard to build my practice to dump it now!" Barrie tried to calm her rising anger. "And what do you care about my work-life balance? I'm competition, that's all."

"You are competition," he said. "And I'd much rather work with you than against you. We're both good vets, Barrie. Together we would service all of this county."

"We could do that separately, too," she replied. "If you were so interested in working with me, you'd offer to be partners—fifty-fifty."

"No." He barked out a bitter laugh. "I've been at this for thirty years. You've been on your own for what... three years?"

"Four."

"Four years," he conceded. "Does that seem fair to you, that I should share everything down the middle after having built up my own practice all this time?"

"I really have no interest in working *for* you," she said. "I'm sorry. I like being my own boss, and I'm not willing to give that up."

"Fine," he said. "Fair enough. Don't say I didn't offer."

There was something both final and cautionary in his tone, and Barrie's senses tingled. This was more than a passing offer. She could feel it.

"Does this have to do with the building I lease?" she asked.

He was silent for a moment. "I'm buying it, Barrie."

"I heard," she said. "So what's the plan there? Are you going to push me out of my office space?"

"I'm planning on opening a second clinic," he said. "I wanted you to be my assistant vet. You'd be able to stay where you are and I'd give you a cut in your current lease."

"Assistant vet…" she murmured.

"Yes."

She sighed. The cut in her lease was tempting, but working under Palmer Berton again…she just couldn't do it!

"Thank you for thinking of me, but it's too hard to go back to working for someone else, Palmer. I'm sure you can understand that."

"You really can't humble yourself to work for me?" he asked incredulously.

"Humble myself?" she snapped. "Would you have given up your practice four years in?"

"I wasn't a single parent," he said, his voice quiet. "Your situation is different from mine. You should give this some serious thought."

She wanted to find her own solution, but she had a suspicion that wasn't going to be so easy. Palmer Berton had confirmed that he was buying her clinic space, which was good information to have, but now she was backed into a corner. She'd have to find a new space to lease and renovate it to suit her purposes all before the baby was born. And then what? He had a point. None of this would be easy. She'd been hoping to build herself up enough that she could survive without the emergency calls, but what if she couldn't? Dr. Berton expanding to two offices might affect her ability to do so. She still didn't have a solution for all of the changes coming up. Dr. Berton's offer was actually logical. Except she hadn't worked this hard for this long to just give up her autonomy.

"Dr. Berton," she said at last. "I appreciate the offer, and I can see the benefits of your plan. I'm not turning you down because I'm angry or dislike you. This isn't personal. This is about my practice, and that's personal in a whole different way. I'm determined to stay afloat on my own."

"You're sure?"

Was this just a little bit of pride getting in her way? Possibly. "I'm sure. But thank you for the offer."

"Alright then." Dr. Berton sighed. "I'll be in touch when the sale is final, and we can hammer out the details for your exit."

Was she an idiot for holding out, hoping for some solution to present itself? But she knew that she'd regret it more if she agreed to something prematurely and discovered later that she could have kept her own practice intact. That would hurt a whole lot more.

"I suppose there is no way around that," she said. "Have a good night."

She hung up the phone and tossed it onto her bedside table. Miley sat down in front of her and leaned his large head into her lap, soulful eyes looking up at her. Dr. Berton didn't need to do this. He already ran his own practice. He didn't need to expand to swallow her little corner of the business, too, yet he was doing it.

"Blast," she muttered and sucked in a shaky breath. She smoothed a hand over Miley's head and gave him a sad smile.

"I didn't work this hard to lose it, Miley," she said,

and Miley looked back at her in silence. She liked things planned and predictable. She liked to know what was coming and be prepared for the worst. Ironically, that was exactly what Dr. Berton was offering her—stability. But she just couldn't work for him. She still had her pride.

THE NEXT EVENING, Curtis stopped off at the Honky Tonk for a beer. It was located in the west end of town—a short, dumpy building with a neon sign that flickered and buzzed in a blacked out window. He didn't come to the bar often; in fact, he hadn't been here since he'd arrived back in Hope, but he needed some space to himself, and the Honky Tonk seemed like the place to get it.

Curtis ordered himself a beer—his limit, since he'd be driving later—and headed toward the back of the bar, which was a little less populated. A few Christmas decorations were up—a faded wreath on one wall, some garland hung in loops along the front counter. A green felt pool table had a few cowboys surrounding it, and across from the pool table were a dartboard and a couple of old guys playing. Their aim was remarkably good for their level of inebriation. The Honky Tonk was the kind of place that was depressing if you weren't already half in the bag, and the last fifteen years hadn't improved it.

In fact, back when he'd been married, Barrie had made him promise that he wouldn't go there. Controlling, his friends had called it, but he'd understood her fear. All too many guys drank away their paychecks in the Honky Tonk, then went home to their wives with their tails between their legs. Curtis had never wanted to be one of them. It had been one of his and Barrie's deals—marriage being full of deals, he'd found out. Sitting here now still felt like a betrayal to her, but he wasn't sure why. He wasn't her husband and he owed her nothing when it came to his leisure time or his paychecks.

Curtis sat near the back, his beer in front of him and his elbows on the table. The jukebox played a mournful holiday tune about a cowboy grieving a lost love, which wasn't doing much for his mood right now. He hadn't expected to feel that strongly about Barrie—not after all these years. He was no longer the hot-headed cowboy with six-pack abs. And she was no longer the slim girl with the shining eyes. They were both older, and in his case, a little more beaten up. But the sensation of her body pulled hard against his was so sharp in his memory that his heart sped up even thinking about it. She was softer now, rounder, and very obviously pregnant. She was attractive in a whole new way that fired his blood up like some young buck. He knew better than to go there again, so what had happened?

Barrie was still the same woman who hadn't been able to trust him with her future. Nothing had changed there. Except, she'd had a point—what about her career? They could have sorted out something between them, but staying with him, she'd never have achieved quite so much. He didn't like that thought—he'd wanted to give her more, not hold her back. If anything, she'd only proved herself right. She was better off without him—definitely more successful than he'd turned out to be. Maybe that should prove something to him, too, but she was also still the same woman who could turn his logical mind to mush just by being close enough to let him smell her perfume.

And he'd kissed her... She'd kissed him first, but he didn't have to take over quite so thoroughly. He could have given her a quick peck and headed on out, but once her lips had touched his, there was no going back. He'd wanted to do that for far too long now. He wished he could say that the kiss had gotten it out of his system, but it had only whetted his appetite.

Curtis let his gaze move around the bar, and he recognized a couple of guys from high school. Dwight Petersen was there—looking scruffy and sweaty. Curtis wasn't in any rush to reintroduce himself—he'd come here for some quiet, after all—but the drunk cowboy's words were filtering across the bar.

"Dakota never loved Andy," Dwight was saying, his words slurred. "She married him for the money."

"I don't know, man," the fellow sitting next to him said with a shake of his head. "They seem good together."

"He was my best friend!" Dwight was getting emotional now. "A guy doesn't move in on another guy's woman!"

"Yeah, yeah..."

The tabletop in front of the two men was strewn with empty bottles. They'd been at this a while. He wondered how often Dwight had gone over this same sob story. Dakota was now happily married to Andy—Dwight might want to let it go already.

"You got to just move on," the other man said, setting his drink down with a clunk. "Just...just...move on!"

Amen, buddy, Curtis thought ruefully. Sage advice from a drunk guy. Moving on wasn't so easy when a guy's heart was in the wringer, though.

The two men hashed over the unfairness of it all for a few more minutes, and then there seemed to be a change of topic.

"You know who I'd do?" Dwight's tone turned slimy. Curtis grimaced. Did Dwight have any idea how disgusting he sounded or how far his voice carried?

"Who?" The friend was all ears now and Curtis looked away.

"That hot little vet." Dwight laughed coarsely. "We were friends a long time ago. Ran in the same circles. She was hot then, and she's hot now. Legs up to here and…" He continued with a lengthy, detailed description of her body—or at least, what he imagined it to look like. Curtis clenched his teeth and glared in Dwight's direction.

"She don't want you." The friend guffawed.

"I say she does." Dwight leaned toward his friend. "I see the way she looks at me. She always did have a thing for me. And the next time I see her, I'm going to—" He made a grotesque motion with one hand and laughed loudly.

This was just drunken talk—at least that's what Curtis wanted to believe, but he didn't like the sound of what Dwight was blathering on about. Barrie never had a "thing" for Dwight, but that wasn't what grated on him. This wasn't just some unknown woman. This was Barrie…pregnant and vulnerable Barrie, who Dwight was promising to manhandle like a piece of meat. The thought was infuriating.

"She's pregnant, though," the friend said. Even drunk, he seemed to have a moral fiber in there somewhere.

"Single, though," Dwight countered. "And I heard what she likes—"

There was more talk that made Curtis's blood simmer—descriptions of all sorts of sordid things that Dwight was positive Barrie would appreciate, and Curtis clenched his fists so hard that he heard his knuckles pop.

"I'm telling you, she'd want it," Dwight went on. "She might say no, but I'd do unforgivable things to that woman—"

That was all Curtis could handle, and he rose to his feet and took three slow steps toward the other table, his boots thunking loudly against the wood floor. He slammed his bottle down on the scratched tabletop with a bang.

"Evening, Dwight," he growled.

Dwight blinked up at him. "Hey."

"You're talking pretty loudly there."

"So?" Dwight snapped. "What's it to you?"

"I don't like how you're talking," Curtis replied, keeping his voice low. "You mind keeping that filth to yourself?"

"What, about that hot vet?" Dwight asked with a laugh. "What do you care?" The man paused and squinted. "Wait... Curtis Porter?"

"One and the same." Curtis bared his teeth in what he

meant to be a chilly smile, but he wasn't sure he managed even that much.

"No offense, man," Dwight said, the color draining from his face.

"I mean it—shut your mouth about her," Curtis growled.

Dwight was silent for a moment, then frowned. "It's not like you want her. What do you care?"

Drunken logic never ran smooth, and Curtis shook his head. "Don't push this, Dwight. You're drunk. Maybe it's time you went home."

"Even if she begs me for it?" Dwight sneered. He lifted his hand in the grotesque gesture once more, and Curtis grabbed the man's middle finger and bent it back until the oily grin on Dwight's face evaporated into a grimace of pain.

"Hey, leave him alone!" the friend bellowed, rising to his feet, his chair clattering behind him. The man pulled out something that glinted in the low light, and Curtis's first thought was of a blade. He couldn't be sure, but he wasn't working with rational thought right now. It was instinct.

Curtis put out an elbow. It caught the other man in the chin with a hollow sound not unlike a dropped melon, and when Dwight jerked his hand free and bounded to his feet, Curtis had no choice. Dwight's fist was already coming toward him. Curtis dodged the drunken blow and landed one of his own.

The fight was on, he realized dismally, and he could either fight back or get himself beaten to a pulp. Considering his mood right now and the way Dwight had been

talking about Barrie, he opted for the first choice—
much preferable. Besides, on the off chance that Dwight
had been serious about assaulting a woman, he'd make
sure he dissuaded the moron from ever thinking about
it again.

"Call the cops!" Curtis heard someone bellow just as
a punch landed on the side of his head, sending him to
the ground in a cloud of stars. He was up again a moment later, dizzy, but able to block another blow and
deliver a solid punch of his own. He watched his hand
connect with Dwight's face in the most satisfying way,
and the smaller man crumpled to the ground. That one
was for Barrie.

Then something else hit him from behind and there
was a blaze of stars once more.

Dammit...was his last thought before he lost con-
sciousness.

Chapter Ten

Barrie awoke to the sound of her cell phone ringing from the bedside table, and she shot out a hand and groped around until she connected with it. Her body felt like it was filled with cement, but her mind was already trying to focus. She got emergency calls on a regular basis, so she was already pushing past the fog of sleep, wondering what might be the issue. She opened her eyes enough to see the screen and picked up the call.

"Dr. Jones," she said.

"Barrie, this is Detective Mike Cruise at the Hope sheriff's office. I'm sorry to wake you."

Mike—Mallory's sheriff husband?

"It's fine…" She rubbed her free hand over her eyes. "Hi, Mike. What's the problem? Is everything okay?"

"We have your ex-husband in custody, and he gave us your number," Mike replied.

The detective's words slowly sank into her mind, and she squinted at the clock beside her bed. It was past midnight. "You have Curtis at the sheriff's office?" She was awake now, and she pushed herself up onto her elbow. "What happened?"

"He was arrested in an altercation at the Honky Tonk" came the reply. "Are you willing to pick him up?" There was a pause and a murmur in the background. "Mr. Porter asks that you be told that he wasn't drunk."

That sounded like a drunk Curtis thing to say.

"So *was* he drunk, or not?" she demanded. "What happened?"

"No, he wasn't. His alcohol levels were within the legal limits, but he was arrested for assault and battery." Mike's voice softened. "You don't have to come, Barrie. I can drop him off at Betty's place after my shift tonight. Thing is, he's refusing medical attention, and I'd rather not have him bleed all over my cruiser, if it's all the same…"

Mike had always had a dry sense of humor and Barrie shook her head. Some things didn't change—like the rebel bull rider who lived for adventure. But a bar fight? And here she'd been lying in bed last night, wondering about that kiss, wondering if fifteen years had changed anything in Curtis. Apparently, not enough!

"Is he okay?" she asked reluctantly.

"More or less," Detective Cruise replied. "But I'm not willing to just release him on his own right now. He needs more TLC than I'm willing to provide at the moment."

So he was roughed up, too. She sighed. "Okay. I won't be long."

"Thanks, Barrie," Mike replied. "I'm sorry about this."

"Is isn't your fault, Mike," she said. "See you soon."

Barrie hung up the phone and swung her legs over

the side of her bed. Curtis at the sheriff's office in the middle of the night… He'd always been impetuous, and this was the reason she'd made him promise that he'd never go back to the Honky Tonk—she didn't want this life, and she'd seen it too often in her own extended family. She had an uncle who drank his family into the poorhouse, and a few cousins who did the same. She'd seen it all up close and personal.

Her alarm at being woken up by a call from the sheriff's office was quickly melting into anger as she pulled on her clothes. Miley didn't even move from his spot on the end of her bed. He lay with his head drooping over one edge and his tail flopping off the other, and he didn't look inclined to get up.

"Miley," she said, patting his rear as she passed him to grab her sweater. "Let's go. You're coming with me."

Miley made a groaning noise, then stretched so that his long legs moved into the center of the bed. Yes, it looked wonderfully comfortable, but if Barrie had to go outside into the cold at midnight, then so did Miley. Fair was fair.

"Come on, lazy bones," she said as she pulled the sweater over her belly. "I need your gallant protection."

Barrie headed out of the bedroom and toward the door, and she heard the sound of Miley's reluctant feet hitting the floor mingled with the jangle of his collar. Miley might not like his slumber disturbed, but his loyalty outweighed his comfort. By the time Barrie had her boots and coat on, Miley was waiting by her side.

Luckily she'd picked up her truck that morning— ready just as the mechanic had promised. The drive to the sheriff's office was short, and after she'd parked, she held open the door for Miley to accompany her. If she was being dragged from her bed at midnight, then the sheriffs could deal with a non-therapy dog in the precinct.

"Hi, Barrie," Mike said as she came through the front door.

"Hi." Barrie nodded toward Miley. "I hope you don't mind, but I didn't want to leave him in the cold."

"No problem." Mike held out his hand, and she shook it. "Mallory's going to kill me for even calling you for this."

Barrie smiled wanly. "She might. So where is he?"

"In the interview room."

"Miley, sit." She turned to her dog and took his large face between her hands. "Stay."

Miley lowered himself onto his haunches, and Barrie followed Mike past the desks, where a couple of officers were typing away on their computers, and the coffee machine, which smelled like the last pot had burned. The interview room was toward the back of the station, and her heart sped up as Mike gripped the knob, then turned back to her.

"He's not pretty," Mike apologized. "And that isn't my fault. I wanted to bring him to the hospital."

"Okay." She nodded. How bad was it that Mike felt the need to warn her?

Mike opened the door then stepped back. As Barrie entered the fluorescent-lit room, she spotted Curtis, a towel and an ice pack held to one side of his face. When he saw Barrie, he grimaced.

"Hi," he said.

Barrie dropped her purse on a table and crossed the room. "Let me see."

"It's not too bad," Curtis said.

"Mike disagrees," she replied. "Show me."

Curtis eased the towel off his face, revealing an eye swollen painfully and a gash above it that had already been butterfly stitched by Mike, she assumed. Her stomach flipped, and she looked away for a moment. She hadn't expected to feel like this. She was a vet— she saw gross and painful injuries on a regular basis.

"I'm fine," Curtis growled. "It'll heal."

"You are not fine, Curtis!" A sob rose in her chest. "What were you thinking?"

She'd been prepared for anger, not for the urge to sit down and cry. She was blaming this on the pregnancy.

"I wasn't drunk."

"A point in your favor," she snapped. "Sort of! So you managed this *sober*?"

"There were extenuating circumstances," he replied, pushing himself to his feet. "Thanks for coming, Barrie. I didn't want to give them anyone's number, but Detective Cruise there insisted, if I wanted to be let out of here."

Barrie glanced back. Mike had left the room, and they were in relative privacy.

"Mike says you should have gone to the hospital," she said.

"Barrie, I've gotten some nasty injuries riding bulls," he said with a sigh. "I have a pretty good sense of when I'm hurt or not. This is cosmetic. It'll heal."

He was just as stubborn as he'd always been—the

same old Curtis. So why couldn't she put aside the way he made her feel?

"So, what was this about?" she asked.

"Dwight Petersen," he replied. "You don't want to know."

"I just got up in the middle of the night to pick you up from the sheriff's station. I absolutely do want to know," she retorted.

Curtis picked up his jacket and winced as he attempted to pull it on. So it wasn't just his face. She put a hand on his arm to stop him and felt down his ribs. Curtis grimaced as she got to a puffy place on his side. A cracked rib, too, no doubt. Broken ribs felt the same on animals as they did on people.

"Dwight Petersen had a few things to say about you," Curtis said, catching her wrist to stop her probing. "And I didn't like it."

"What things?" she asked, pulling her hand free of his grasp.

"Things I don't care to repeat," he said, but she caught the glimmer of disgust in Curtis's dark eyes. Had it been that bad?

"So you started a fight?" she asked.

"I didn't start anything. Okay…maybe I was the first to lay a hand on the slimy twit, but if he ever considered acting on the ugly things he was saying, I wanted him to associate that with a little pain."

"What did he say?" Wariness wormed up inside her.

"He was describing an assault," Curtis replied grimly. "Stay clear of him."

"Oh…" She licked her lips, her bravado slipping away. "Where is he now?"

"He went to the hospital," Curtis replied. "Mike says he'll keep an eye on him. He's definitely on their radar now."

Did that mean that Dwight was in worse shape than Curtis? And was she hoping so?

"For the record, I wasn't the one who beat him so badly. Apparently there were other guys who had a beef with him, too. I was already knocked out cold when they got to Dwight."

That did make her feel a little better, actually. The thought of Curtis beating on some man—deservedly or not—was enough to turn her stomach.

"So you didn't hurt him?" She heard the tremor in her own voice.

"Not very much." He smiled down at her, then grimaced in pain. "I got in one solid right hook. That's it."

"I never liked the Honky Tonk," she said.

"I know." Curtis reached forward and brushed a tendril of hair away from her face. "I'm sorry about this, Barrie. I had to give them a number or end up in a cell tonight. Maybe I should have taken the cell."

"No." She sighed. "Come on. I'll take you back to my place and get you cleaned up. You can sleep on my couch tonight, if you want."

"I don't need babying," he said. "If you'd just drop me off at my truck, I can take it from there."

Curtis might not want babying, but he hadn't grown up much in the last fifteen years. If he had changed, he wouldn't have been in the bar to begin with, and he'd never have let himself get goaded into some stupid fight.

Barrie shot Curtis a disappointed look as he eased into the cab of her SUV. Yeah, that was familiar. Miley jumped into the back seat, and she slammed the door. He leaned over to push the driver's side door open, and a stab of pain shot through his ribs.

"I always hated this," Barrie said as she hoisted herself into the driver's seat, ignoring his grunt of pain as he pulled himself into an upright position again.

"This is my first bar brawl," he replied with a small smile.

"I hated picking you up with broken ribs, a cast, a split lip…" She turned the key and the engine rumbled to life. "But it was your choice. You loved bull riding, and nothing I ever said could keep you from it."

"This was a little different," he said.

"Not to me." She pulled out of the parking lot and onto Montana Avenue. "This is exactly the same from where I'm sitting. I get a call, and I come pick you up in pieces."

"Barrie, I'm fine." Curtis heaved an irritated sigh. "I get that I'm not pretty right now, but a cold steak on this eye and I'll be presentable."

Barrie didn't answer, and Curtis turned his attention to the streets sliding past. He knew her well enough to see that under that veneer of anger was fear. This had scared her—and, well, it should. A fight hadn't been his intention, but if he could redo tonight, he couldn't say that he'd do anything differently. She hadn't heard the things Dwight had said, and if Curtis had his way, she never would. That would scare her a whole lot more than his mangled mug. They were approaching the turn for the Honky Tonk, but she didn't seem to be slowing down.

"My truck is in the bar parking lot," he said.

"Hmm." She passed the turn without even a glance.

"So you're not dropping me off at my truck," he clarified.

"You're coming home with me," she replied, her tone icy.

"You don't have to do this," he said.

"I really *shouldn't* have to do this!" Barrie shot him an angry look. "I'm taking you back to my place and giving you that cold steak for your eye. If you want your truck so badly tonight, you can damn well walk to the Honky Tonk, but I'm not leaving you there."

Curtis wasn't sure how to answer that—this was a Barrie he'd never seen before. Back in their married days, she'd have yelled and cried. She'd even kicked him out a couple of times. But whatever lecture might have been coming his way back then didn't seem forthcoming now. It stood to reason—they were no longer married. But taking him back to her place was no longer necessary, either.

Barrie signaled the turn onto her street.

"I appreciate the gesture," he said. "But I'm not exactly helpless here."

Barrie pulled into her drive and parked. Then she turned toward him. "So I'm supposed to just not worry about you, then? I should just crawl back into my bed and forget all about you?"

"It's what most exes do."

"I guess I'm not like most." She got out of the truck and slammed her door. Curtis looked back at Miley, who met Curtis's gaze with a mournful look of his own.

"Women, am I right?" Curtis muttered.

Then Barrie pulled open the back door to let Miley out. The dog looked between Curtis and his mistress, then scrambled down and into the snow. Curtis opened his own door and headed around the vehicle. Barrie hadn't waited for him, and she stood with her back to him while she unlocked the front door. Miley was marking a bush at the side of the house.

"Come on," Barrie said, her tone softening, and when he and Miley both moved toward her, he suddenly wondered which one of them she'd been talking to. Whatever. He'd take her up on that offer of a cold steak, and after that, he'd leave her alone.

When Curtis got inside, he managed to ease out of his coat without any help. Those ribs were bruised, not broken—he knew the difference from experience. Bull riding was harder on a body than bar brawls.

"Sit," Barrie ordered, pulling out a kitchen chair.

Miley dropped into a seated position, and the dog shot Curtis a sidelong look.

"He seems to know when you're serious." Curtis chuckled, and he headed for the chair that Barrie indicated.

"Not you, silly," Barrie said, rubbing her hand over

Miley's head. Then she went to the fridge and pulled out a bowl of fresh meat cuts.

"So you just have beef in your fridge all the time?" he asked incredulously.

"It's Miley's, so yes," she said, picking through the bowl until she came up with a marbled, gristly piece of meat that looked big enough. Then she came over to where he sat and looked down on him. Her eyes had lost the angry glitter, leaving her looking tired and sad.

"You sure you don't want to just yell at me like the good old days?" he asked testily. Honestly, it would have been easier to tune her out if she'd just tell him off.

"I think we're past that, aren't we?" She carefully laid the meat over his swollen eye. "There."

Miley, still seated, eyed the meat on Curtis's face covetously. Barrie took another couple of pieces of meat to Miley's bowl and dropped them in. Miley followed and gulped them down in two mouthfuls.

"Why did you like it so much?" she asked after a moment of silence. "The bull riding, I mean."

"Adrenaline," he replied. "It makes you feel alive— man against beast." Not unlike a bar fight with Dwight, ironically enough.

"Hmm." She turned on the tap and washed her hands. "And that was enough to endure the broken bones and concussions and—" she turned the water off "—the pain?"

"I survived." He attempted to turn and look at her, but his side was too sore to allow the twisting motion.

"You never did think of what it did to me, did you?" She pulled out the chair opposite him, then sank into it. "Do you know what it's like to see the man you love in that state?"

"It's part of the sport, Barrie—"

"I know, I know." She sighed. "And it's no longer my business. But all of this—" she gestured to his face "—is a little too familiar."

Her sitting in the kitchen late at night, looking pale and drawn—yeah, this was pretty familiar to him, too. Them butting heads over what he wanted, and what she wanted... It was exhausting.

"I wasn't trying to hurt you back then," he said. "I needed the outlet. I mean, I was no good at school, and bull riding was the one thing that people gave me some credit for. I needed that. You were smart, going places. Everyone said so. I was—" He shrugged, unsure of how to finish that. He was the guy no one thought was good enough for the likes of Barrie Jones.

"You were smart, too," she countered.

Curtis didn't answer. He didn't need to be soothed or mollycoddled. He knew the score, and he'd made his peace with it over the years. Some guys were better at book work, and some guys had better instincts with hands-on work. Curtis was the latter, and that eight-second ride was his proof. That was the one place that his skill set—agility, instinct and bullheaded courage—seemed to matter. Because it sure hadn't been enough to keep him married.

"I loved you, Curtis." She sighed softly. "I really did. And every time you came home with a broken bone or a nasty sprain, it meant that you were choosing an eight-second thrill over me."

"You had me for life, Barrie. You couldn't give me eight seconds?"

"It's my fault, really." Barrie pushed herself to her feet, one hand in the small of her back. "I thought I could tame you."

She started to move past him again, and he shot out his hand and caught her wrist. "You did."

"I thought you'd turn into a family man," she said. "I thought you'd come home to me in the evenings, and we'd talk and cuddle. I thought you'd become a husband and maybe—" she tugged her wrist free of his grasp "—and maybe a father."

Curtis dropped his hand. "I wasn't ready to be a dad back then. I told you that all the time."

"I know."

That had been a source of arguments, too. She wanted a baby right away. That was before she changed her mind and decided she wanted school first. They'd both been young, and she hadn't found her path yet, apparently. For Curtis, he'd wanted to have some fun. Just because they were married didn't mean they had to start with all the heavy responsibilities so soon. They were young and healthy and in love... Frankly, he was more concerned about his time with her between the sheets than he was with starting a family.

"A baby wouldn't have made things easier between us," he added.

"I know that, too." She smiled tiredly. "And you want to know something? I was dumb enough back then to think that a baby would nail you down with us, give you another reason to drop the bull riding and do something serious."

"Yeah?" He'd suspected as much, but he was surprised to hear her admit to it. She went back to the counter and flicked on the electric kettle. Her voice came from behind him, so he couldn't see her face.

"I've done a lot of thinking about it over the years, and I realized that while I loved you for who you were, I wanted to marry you for your potential to be...more. And that doesn't work. I was trying to change you into a different man, and I thought that marriage *would* change you."

Which was why she never should have married him to begin with. He heard that loud and clear. And while he could agree on a logical, mental level, his heart ached.

"I always was too stubborn for my own good," he said.

"Yes, you were." She came back and sat down again.

"I think we both had an idea of what marriage would be, and we never really talked about it," he said. "Or maybe we already knew that if we put all our cards on the table it wouldn't work."

"Maybe," she said. "Everyone told us to think it through, and we were determined to plow ahead anyway."

More than determined. Desperate. All he'd wanted was to make it legal, claim her as his... If only he'd known how hard marriage would turn out to be. Love wasn't enough when building a life with a woman.

"I might have been a stubborn lout, but for what it's worth, I loved you."

She smiled sadly, then dropped her gaze to the table. "I know."

Of all the tangle of things he wished he could tell her, that was the most important. They might have been mismatched from the start, but he'd been there for the right reasons. The kettle started to whistle, breaking the moment.

"Do you want tea?" she asked.

"No, thanks." He pulled the piece of meat off his eye. "What I want is for you to go to bed and get some rest. I feel bad enough having woken you up."

"I can make you a bed on the couch," she said.

"No." That's where this ended. He wasn't a bedraggled kitten to be cared for by Barrie's big heart. Besides, if he had to spend the night a stone's throw from her bedroom, she'd either end up kicking him out, or he'd convince her to do something they'd both regret the next morning. "I'm going to walk over to the Honky Tonk and pick up my truck."

"But you're—"

"I'm fine," he interrupted her. "Look." He could feel that the swelling on his eye had gone down already.

Barrie put out one hand and gingerly touched his temple. Her fingers lingered, and Curtis put a hand over hers. Looking at her—her eyes bleary with exhaustion, her hair mussed and her belly domed out in front of her—he wanted to be the one to take care of her, not the other way around. He wanted to pull her into his arms and prove just how "fine" he really was, and that mental image was so strong, he had to shut his eyes to vanquish it. He'd already let things go too far in this kitchen once already, and he wasn't going to do that again.

"I'll get going," he said, and he rose to his feet.

This time when he went to the door, he kept his hands to his sides. "Thank you, Barrie."

He meant for tonight, for fifteen years ago when she'd shared her life with him for just a short while… for enduring the frustration that came with an emotionally stunted bull rider.

"Don't mention it."

Curtis settled his hat back on his head and opened the door. He'd get his truck and go back to the ranch. Chores would be waiting at 4:00 a.m. whether he was ready or not. And he needed to think clearly. Frustrating as it was, Barrie still seemed capable of firing his blood without any effort on her part.

Chapter Eleven

Barrie stood in her kitchen the next morning, a mug of tea on the counter next to a stack of buttered toast. It was Saturday, and her clinic was closed, except for emergency calls. She was glad for the quiet and the time to herself. She'd slept in after her late night with Curtis, and she'd woken up feeling restless and uncertain.

Curtis was getting under her skin again, and she hated that. They'd always had an unexplainable chemistry. Even when she'd been furious with him last night, she'd felt it—that desire to take care of him, clean him up, give him some comfort.

"Miley, that man isn't my problem anymore," she said, carrying the tea and toast to the table. "You'd think I could remember that."

Miley followed her, his eyes pinned to her plate of toast. She chuckled and tore off a crust for him, which he swallowed in one gulp.

But Curtis had felt it, too, last night. She'd seen that hungry look in his eye and the dogged determination to keep it in check. She knew his tells, and when his jaw tensed and his gaze grew laser focused, she knew what he was thinking. The realization sent shivers through her. The physical aspect of their relationship had always been amazing. He could coax pleasure out of her that she hadn't even known was possible. But she pushed those memories back. Their sensual connection hadn't been enough to save their marriage, and it wasn't enough to start something up again.

He'd been right to leave instead of staying the night. She'd never have slept properly knowing he was out there on the couch. She was as bad as he was when it came to their attraction. Their feelings for each other had always been intense—both the chemistry and the frustration when they just couldn't seem to get on the same page, and she knew better than to toy with impulses that strong.

Barrie's cell phone blipped, and she glanced down at an incoming text from Mallory:

Mike told me about Curtis. What happened?

Long story, she typed back. Too much to text.

How about a little shopping? Mike will take the kids for the morning.

Barrie sighed. Did she really want to do this? She was already wound up about Curtis, and shopping wasn't exactly relaxing... But this might be good for her—get her out of her head a little bit. She picked up the phone and typed back:

Sure. I'll meet you at the store. What time?

An hour later, Barrie arrived at Hope's one and only maternity shop, Blooming Motherhood. Mallory met her on the sidewalk out front, holding two coffees. Mallory's sandy-blond hair was pulled back in a ponytail, and her cheeks were rosy from the cold. She passed a cup to Barrie.

"Really?" Barrie broke into a smile. "Thanks."

"I had a feeling you could use it after last night," Mallory replied. "So how are you?"

"I'm fine," Barrie said, taking a sip of what turned out to be a hazelnut latte. "He's the same guy he's always been, just a bit older. I don't know what to say."

"What happened after you picked him up from the station?" Mallory pressed.

"I took him back to my place and put a steak on his eye, and then he left." Barrie shrugged. "It was all so familiar—bandaging up my broken cowboy... I can't do it anymore."

"But this was different, wasn't it?" Mallory asked. "He wasn't bull riding, at least."

"When he left, I went to bed, and instead of remembering the good times with Curtis, all I could think about was how shredded I felt when he left me. I still remember waking up the next morning after he'd packed his bag and stomped out, and thinking, 'He'll come back. He always comes back.' And I was planning on punishing him a little bit. Maybe being gone when he finally did. Let him feel some of the pain I felt. But..." Barrie shrugged. "That was the last time."

"What did you fight about?" Mallory asked.

"Curtis was offered a chance to do the bull riding circuit," Barrie replied. "We'd been fighting about everything at that point, and when I said forget it, he said that I was controlling. And that stabbed, because I wasn't trying to control him…" Barrie sighed. "Or maybe I was. I wanted to make him into a stable husband, and that wasn't Curtis. Long story short, we both said things that we couldn't take back, and I told him to get out. And he did."

Barrie's eyes misted and she shook her head. "You see? This is stupid! It was fifteen years ago, but seeing him again has been harder than I thought."

Mallory reached out and squeezed Barrie's hand. "We never quite forget the ones that got away, do we?"

"Apparently not," Barrie agreed. "But it was for the best. If he was going to leave me, better sooner than later, I guess." She hadn't intended to get into all of this on the street, and her cheeks flushed. "Let's go in. I'm cold."

Once they were inside, the shopkeeper called out a cheery hello. Barrie looked around at the various pregnant mannequins and heaved a sigh. She didn't know where to start. Before this belly, she knew what she liked—jeans, fitted tees and the odd sweater. But even her largest sweaters were starting to get snug.

"What about this?" Mallory asked, holding up a shirt.

Barrie eyed it for a moment, not sure what to think. Mallory's expression softened, and she stepped closer. "Do you hate it? Like it? I need a reaction here."

Barrie shrugged. "I don't even know."

"You look like you're hiding, Barrie."

"What?" Barrie looked from the shirt to her friend.

"Your pregnancy," Mallory clarified. "You look like you're trying to hide it instead of celebrate it. And I know all about that. I tried to hide my pregnancy with Beau until the last possible minute. If I could undo that, I would. You deserve to enjoy this."

"This town doesn't want to celebrate this baby," Barrie replied, her voice low. "I'm the scandal, remember?"

"You're pregnant, you're beautiful and this baby is already loved," Mallory replied, meeting her gaze. "Dress like it."

Her friend was right. She might not feel like flaunting this pregnancy, but she did love her baby already, and her child deserved to be celebrated by her, at the very least. Barrie looked around at the various styles of shirts, and she spotted a fitted striped sweater with a cowl neck that looked cozy and soft. "I like that."

"Good." Mallory went and grabbed one from the rack. "What about this one?"

They picked out a few tops together, then snagged a few pairs of maternity jeans that Barrie had to admit looked a whole lot more comfortable than the low-waisted jeans she was wearing now. The saleswoman gladly put everything aside in a changing room.

"Mike couldn't tell me what happened to Curtis, exactly," Mallory said. "Privacy issues and all that. I know there was a fight at the bar, but that's about it."

"Apparently, Dwight Petersen was saying some horrible things about me," Barrie replied.

"And Curtis stood up for you," her friend concluded.

"It wasn't necessary," she said. She wasn't Curtis's wife anymore, and he didn't get to be all territorial about her. Except she'd gotten the impression that this hadn't just been male ego… Curtis had been scared for her.

"And if he'd just sat there and let him?" Mallory countered.

"I'd never have been the wiser," she replied. "And I'd probably have been happier that way."

"Dwight is a scary guy," Mallory said quietly. "He's angry—like, deep down angry. Mike says I need to stay away from him, too, and Mike doesn't say that kind of thing without good reason. I don't know, Barrie. Maybe it's better that Curtis did something."

Barrie sighed. "I'm more upset with myself, Mal. I kissed him."

"Who?" Mallory gasped.

"Curtis." She shot her friend an incredulous smile. "And it was on me. He'd rubbed my feet, and made me a meal and I guess it just felt really good to be cared for—"

"Was this before or after the bar fight?" Mallory asked.

"Before, which is why that fight is so annoying. I'm not his anymore, and he can't act like I am. One ill-advised kiss doesn't change that."

"Is it possible that old feelings are coming back?"

"And what if they did?" Barrie shook her head. "It doesn't change anything. Mal, I'm having a baby. Babies need stability…and so do I. And Curtis was always the kind of guy who thought stability was boring. If I'm going to have a man in my life, he needs to be someone I can rely on, because I don't have enough strength to be taking care of an impulsive man as well as myself and a newborn. Heck, I didn't have the strength for it when it was only me."

"And he hasn't grown up at all?" Mallory asked. "Fifteen years is a long time. Everyone changes."

"See that's my problem—" Barrie tugged her hair out of her face. "I married him the first time for his potential. I could see the man he could be if he only tried. Just because a man could be something doesn't mean he wants to be. I'm not making that mistake twice."

"No, I hear you there," Mallory agreed. "I'm sorry, Barrie. This can't be easy."

"It's just bad timing," Barrie said. "I'm having a baby and I'm trying to figure out how I'll run my practice and be a mom at the same time. Curtis is selling the building I'm leasing, and Palmer Berton is pushing for me to work for him again... If it weren't for these hormones coursing through my system, I'm sure I'd be a lot more levelheaded."

Except she wasn't actually sure of that. Curtis had always been her weakness, and he still was, despite everything else that was tipping her world.

Barrie stopped when she saw a party dress that was so beautiful she could hardly imagine wearing it. It was crimson, with a satiny crisscross top that would accentuate her bust and a soft, flowing skirt that would swirl around her legs at a tea length.

"For my party?" Mallory asked hopefully. "You've got the legs for it, Barrie. Not all of us do!"

"I don't know…" Barrie hesitated.

"It's on sale, too!" Mallory turned around the tag and Barrie took a closer look. "Try it on…"

Maybe Mallory was right. It would be nice to feel pretty again, put together. Barrie met her friend's gaze, then smiled. "Alright. I'll splurge for your party."

CURTIS COULDN'T GET a parking spot in front of Mutt's Fish and Chips on Main Street, and had to settle for a space across the street and south a few yards. His stomach rumbled. He'd expected to eat lunch at the ranch, like usual, but Betty had hurried him off to town to pick up a prescription. Before she'd hustled him out the door, he noticed that she'd put on some makeup.

"Who are you dressing up for?" he'd asked. Her reply was a wrathful glare and a list of items to pick up from town, including her blood pressure prescription, which she'd said she needed because he kept doing stupid things like getting into bar fights. So he'd done what any self-respecting nephew would—apologized once again for his battered face and headed for town. Apparently Betty needed some space.

On his way out, he'd passed Dr. Berton just turning in, and the men had exchanged a somber wave. Curtis rolled down his window.

"Morning," he called.

"Morning," Palmer replied. "You look the worse for wear. What happened?"

"Misunderstanding at the Honky Tonk," Curtis said wryly. "This'll be a hard one to live down."

"Ah." Palmer nodded slowly.

"Just wondering about the inspection," Curtis went on, eager to change the subject. "That happens today, right?"

"They assured me it will," Palmer said. "Don't worry. Everyone is aware of your time constraints for this sale. The lawyers are on it."

"Good to know." Curtis nodded. "Thanks."

"Well, nice to see you." Palmer rolled his window up and, with another wave, drove on past toward the house. Whatever relationship Palmer had with his aunt might not be his business, but Curtis was mighty curious. Their current veterinary needs were being taken care of by Barrie—and his aunt was a stickler for those kinds of proprieties—so was this…social? Betty had mentioned that they were friends, but buddies didn't normally warrant lipstick and mascara…did they?

Curtis had wondered about that all the way into Hope, and after running his errands and tossing a couple of bags into the back of his truck, hunger gnawed at his gut. Since he was apparently not invited to lunch back at the ranch, fish and chips would do nicely. Snow started to fall, big fluffy flakes that spun and drifted on their way down.

He parked his truck and got out, glancing into a shop window as he walked past. It was Blossoming Motherhood—a store he hadn't taken any notice of since his return, but he spotted someone he recognized.

Barrie stood in the shop next to another woman,

three plastic bags over one arm. She was smiling about something, and as she spoke to her friend, she started pulling on a pair of gloves. He was frozen to the spot, watching her while she didn't know she was being observed. There was something about Barrie—a sparkle in her eye when she was honestly amused—that he'd always found intoxicating. Barrie and her friend moved toward the door, and it was then that Barrie looked forward and spotted him. Blast. He looked across the street toward Mutt's Fish and Chips, then back at Barrie as she came outside onto the sidewalk.

"Hey…" he said.

"Curtis…" Barrie glanced toward her friend, who perked up considerably when she heard his name. "This is my friend Mallory—Detective Cruise's wife."

"Ah." Curtis shook her hand. "Nice to meet you. So I guess you've heard about me."

"A bit." Mallory shot Barrie a mildly amused look. "Your face doesn't look as bad as I thought."

"Nice of you to say," Curtis muttered ruefully. "I'll be fine. I didn't mean to interrupt. I'm just headed over for lunch at Mutt's."

"You're hungry, right, Barrie?" Mallory asked. "And I'm just looking at the time here. I promised my husband I wouldn't be too long today, so I should probably get back."

Was that a hint? Barrie licked her lips, giving her friend an unreadable look. Had he been the topic of conversation or something? Probably, considering that Mallory's husband had been the one to arrest him.

"Yeah, well, Barrie, if you want to join me for lunch, it's on me," he said.

"It was great seeing you, girl," Mallory said, leaning in to give Barrie a squeeze. "Call me!"

With that, Mallory headed off down the sidewalk. Color rose in Barrie's cheeks.

"She's not too subtle, is she?" Curtis asked with a low laugh.

"She means well." Barrie shook her head. "But don't worry. I'm not going to hold you to that. Have a nice lunch, Curtis. I'll see you—"

"Barrie." He put a hand out to stop her. "I was serious about the offer of lunch. If nothing else, I owe you for pain and suffering last night."

"That was for old times' sake," she said. Then she eyed his face a little more closely. "You don't look half as bad as you did last night."

His eye was bruised around the temple, but the bruises weren't as dark as they could have been.

"Thanks to a timely steak." He smiled. "Look, if you still like fish and chips as much as you used to…"

A small smile tugged at Barrie's lips.

"Come on," he cajoled. "People have been staring at you because of the baby, and now I'm drawing stares for this black eye. Let's give them something to really talk about, and have lunch together." He winked. "What a scandal."

"It's a terrible reason, but Mal was right—I'm starving." She chuckled. "Let's go."

Curtis put a hand on her elbow as they crossed the street. It was only in case she slipped, but he was feeling increasingly protective of Barrie. If she had a guy in her life, he'd have backed off...or would he? He wasn't so sure anymore. Barrie was no longer his, and he knew that whatever they'd been to each other was rooted in the distant past. But seeing her again, fighting with her, standing so close that he could smell her perfume...

"How are your ribs?" Barrie asked, pulling him out of his thoughts.

"A bit sore, but not too bad," he said. "They're only bruised. I told you it wasn't as bad as it looked."

"But you always said that." She ran a hand through her hair. "And you weren't always telling the truth."

Yeah, well, back then he hadn't wanted her to know how bad some of his injuries were—a mixture of male pride and stubbornness. And maybe that hadn't changed. Curtis pulled open the restaurant's front door and suppressed a wince at the jab of pain through his ribs. She passed inside ahead of him. A sign told them to seat themselves, and he spotted a booth next to the front windows.

"Food first," he said, putting a hand on the small of her back and nudging her in the direction of the empty booth. Curtis noticed a few eyes on them as they made their way through the restaurant. A short-lived marriage from fifteen years ago wasn't ancient enough history for the town of Hope to forget. Was it bad that he was enjoying having people jump to conclusions? Barrie lowered herself onto the bench, then slid in and he seated himself opposite her.

"So, Mallory is Mike's wife," Curtis said. He'd known the police officer back when they were all a lot younger, and Mike becoming a cop was pretty surprisingly, actually.

"Mallory was his nanny," Barrie said. "Mike's cousin went to prison and left him with her daughter, Katie. So Mike hired Mallory to help out with childcare, and…" She shrugged. "The rest is history."

"Wow." He nodded. "I'm happy for him. He was a bit of a jerk last night, but—"

"What did he do?" Barrie asked.

"Besides insisting I call someone?" He raised his eyebrows. "Do I have to take all the blame for that late night phone call?"

Barrie rolled her eyes and picked up a menu. "You weren't exactly cooperative about medical care, either, you know."

"You mean not staying put at your place?" he clarified, and her cheeks colored. He'd hit on it. "Barrie, I couldn't… It was a kind offer, but—"

She lifted her eyes to meet his, and the words evaporated on his tongue. How could she still do that? Curtis cleared his throat.

"I'm still a red-blooded male, Barrie," he said.

She smiled slightly, then dropped her gaze. "I wasn't offering anything more than the couch."

"I know that," he said. "But I wasn't going to be able to lie on that couch and know that you were just down a hallway…" He wasn't sure if he should say anything more, but whatever. He wasn't here for much longer anyway. "Whatever it was that had me hooked on you back then hasn't changed. I look at you and…" He heaved a sigh, searching for a way to explain that didn't sound crude. "I can't look away."

She met his gaze once more, but this time her confidence had slipped and he saw uncertainty swirling in her eyes.

"I'm not twenty-two anymore, Curtis," she said quietly. "I've aged. The body that you knew and loved is pretty much gone." She gestured toward her belly. "Pregnancy will do that, even if fifteen years didn't. So yeah, we still feel that draw toward each other, but this is different."

What she didn't seem to realize was that he no longer craved a twenty-two-year-old. He was no young buck, either, and he wasn't scared off by the softening of a few years. She was still gorgeous, and if she saw the accumulation of scars on his body, she might be set at ease. The allure that Barrie wielded wasn't just physical, though. The vows he'd taken on their wedding day had tied him to her in a way that he hadn't fully appreciated as a twenty-year-old kid. He'd walked away and signed those divorce papers, but it hadn't severed everything. He missed *her*.

"I know," he said soberly. "I'm sorry, Barrie. I'm not trying to cross any boundaries, or—"

"But yes." Her words were so soft that he almost didn't hear them.

"Yes?" He leaned forward.

"Yes, I feel it," she said with a small smile. "And from now on, I'll be smart enough to curb it."

Chapter Twelve

The waitress arrived, and Barrie turned her attention back to the menu. The truth was, regardless of their attraction for each other, Curtis was doing what he'd always done—exactly what was best for him.

Curtis ordered a Coke and a plate of fish and chips. His voice was low and familiar, and she hated how her heart tugged toward him. Familiar wasn't necessarily a good thing—he was still the same guy!

Under the table, Curtis's leg stretched out and rested against hers. That was something he used to do years ago—she felt her cheeks warm.

"And for you?" The waitress turned toward her.

"Um." Barrie moved her leg. "I'll have the same, thanks."

The waitress smiled and whisked off again, leaving them in relative privacy. Barrie needed to get this back into safer territory.

"Curtis," she said, keeping her voice low. "There was something that's bothered me all these years."

"Yeah?" He frowned slightly, and his dark gaze met hers.

"You left." Barrie sighed. "I know I kicked you out for, like, the fourth time. I know that was childish on my part, but what…" She swallowed. "Why was that time different?"

Because she hadn't seen it coming. She'd known how much Curtis loved her, and she'd honestly thought that after he'd cooled down, he'd be back and they'd sort something out like they always did. How was she to know that he'd stay away?

"Nothing…" Sadness welled in his eyes. "I know that's hard to hear. I guess it just finally clicked in my head—you didn't want this."

She was silent, her heart pounding. Nothing had been different? So, had their entire marriage been borrowed time?

"When I married you, I had this image of what kind of husband I'd be." His boot scraped as he pulled his leg back. "I'd take care of you. I'd make you proud. I'd make enough money to keep you comfortable, and crawl into bed next to you at night and know that I was home."

That sounded wonderful, but she was afraid to say it. "And…"

"It wasn't like that," he went on. "I felt like a failure, I guess. I gave you everything I had, and when I tried to stretch a bit so I could give you more, you'd get so angry. That night, when I told you I wanted to go on the circuit—go together on that circuit—you got this look on your face like I was nuts, and I suddenly saw myself through your eyes."

"I never thought you were a loser," she said earnestly. "I promise you that."

"I wasn't a provider, though," he said with a shrug. "Not enough of one. You were used to more. And I certainly wasn't measuring up. When I suggested doing something together away from Hope and away from your parents and all those expectations, I could see in your face that you didn't trust me. You needed this town to feel safe, because you didn't feel safe with me."

"I was scared," she said.

"It was more than that." Curtis licked his lips. "I wasn't what I wanted to be... I wanted to be the guy who soothed away your fears. I wanted to be the guy you looked to... I wanted you to hitch your wagon to my star."

Barrie was silent. Had he really wanted all of that? It sounded beautiful now, but their reality hadn't been so idealistic.

"It was a risk, though," she said.

"Yep." He nodded. "And I'm not saying you made a mistake there. I mean, look at you—you've got your life together."

"But you're saying you left because I didn't trust you enough?" she clarified.

"I left because I didn't like who I was with you. I didn't want to be the petty guy who kept pissing you off. I wanted to be a better man, and I just couldn't seem to figure it out." He met her gaze. "And I'm sorry for that. Really sorry. I had to go—we couldn't carry on like we were. I was suffocating."

That word stung, and she winced. Had all of her attempts to create a home for him—for them—been sucking his breath away? If she were honest with herself, she had been trying to tie him down. It hadn't been healthy for either of them, had it?

"I was smothering you…" she whispered.

"I don't blame you, Barrie," he said. "I just wasn't the kind of husband I knew I should be, and I didn't know how to fix myself. I thought if we could get away and do something together, we might find our stride, but I saw the look on your face when I suggested it, and I knew what it meant. I wasn't the man you needed, either."

In a way, he was right—she'd needed more stability, and Curtis had refused to be tamed. He craved adventure, and he wanted her to drop everything and go with him. But a life wasn't built on impetuous choices and seeing where they landed. Lives were built with purposeful steps—at least, that was what she'd always thought.

"I'm sorry," she said quietly.

"Hey—" He cleared his throat. "Me, too. I was too young to recognize that I couldn't be that guy for you."

"So…" She sucked in a breath. "Enough about the past. Tell me about this stud farm."

"You really want to hear about that?" he asked.

She shrugged. "Why not? You obviously believe in it."

"I'm going in fifty-fifty with a friend of mine. He found the listing, actually, and we went out to Wyoming to take a look. It's a pretty new setup, and my buddy knows a thing or two about stud services. The owner is anxious to sell. A nasty divorce, apparently. Anyway, we're the only ones interested, which kept that price affordable. It's a once-in-a-lifetime opportunity."

"You'd be nailed down," she pointed out.

"I'd be in a position to make some good cash." He met her gaze. "And a man needs that."

"Did you ever think of just…keeping my building and sticking around here?" she asked.

"I can't afford it. Your lease only covers some upkeep. That building is a drain. It's only worth something if I sell it. Thing is, if I stick around here, Barrie, I'm just some washed-up bull rider. In Wyoming—"

"Yeah." She could see that. In Wyoming, he'd be someone. Finally. "You deserve that."

"You sure?" He smiled ruefully. "I'm making your life harder."

Barrie was well aware of that, but wasn't this their tension from the beginning? It was him or her. Always had been. The waitress returned with a platter that had several dishes on it. She put their plates on the table in front of them, then moved on to the next table. Barrie looked down at the crispy breaded fish and then back at Curtis.

"I know I said otherwise, Curtis, but I don't regret it."

"Marrying me?" he asked, then laughed softly. "You sure about that?"

"It hurt when it ended," she said. "Horribly. It was the worst thing I've ever endured, and before seeing you again, I would have said that I wished I hadn't married you at all, that I'd skipped that whole experience. But now that I see you again…"

He was silent, and she tried to collect her thoughts. How could she explain this?

"I think we've both come a long way," she said at

last. "And we're okay. We got through it, and we're both capable adults. Sometimes it's a good thing to know how much you can survive."

"I don't want to be the guy you survived," he said, his voice low.

"I didn't mean it like that."

He nodded. "I know. But…for the record."

She smiled and said, "Okay. How about we both survived the marriage? Not each other. We were young and idealistic, and had no idea what to expect. We were victims of romance."

Curtis chuckled. "It's thin ice, but I'll take it."

Barrie picked up a fry and dipped it into her tartar sauce. She was hungry, and they both started to eat. The fish was flaky and moist, and the batter was fried to perfection. The background music was the local radio station, and a jaunty Christmas carol medley came on that brought a smile to Barrie's face.

"Do you think we're mature enough to be friends by now?" Curtis asked, popping a fry into his mouth.

"I think so," she said. "Fresh starts. Forgiveness. Isn't that what Christmas is about?"

He angled his head to one side and plunged his fork into a fish stick. "So you forgive me for having to sell?"

"Not entirely." That was her honest answer.

"What if I did you a favor?" he asked.

"What kind?"

"I'll teach you how to make those shortbread cookies."

"You really know how?" She eyed him skeptically.

"I really know how." He raised an eyebrow. "A truce. A goodbye."

Was he feeling guilty about the sale? Probably, as well he should.

"Alright, that would be nice." Barrie paused. "As for our chemistry—"

"I'll behave." He shot her a grin, and when she didn't answer, he said, "It's possible, you know."

But she wasn't only worried about Curtis… This mature version of the boy who'd stolen her heart was more dangerous. If she let herself feel too much for him, she'd fall again…and if there was one thing Barrie had learned, it was that she didn't bounce back very well. She crawled out and clawed her way forward, but there was very little bounce and a lot of pain. This time, she had a child to consider, and she had to keep her heart firmly in check.

"Are you free tonight?" Curtis asked.

Tonight was Mallory's Christmas party, and she was glad to have an excuse. She needed some distance from Curtis, some space to get her emotions untangled again.

"I can't," she said. "I've got plans."

Curtis picked up another fry. "Fair enough. But before I leave."

Barrie cut into the flaky fish with the side of her fork. He knew how to tempt her—but those cookies were about more than time with him. She wanted to master that recipe to feel in control. And yes, she recognized that he was her weakness, but she needed this. Curtis was on his way out, and she and her baby would be on their own. At the very least, she'd be able to bake a delicious buttery cookie and decorate it for every occasion. Then she could feel more confident that she was ready to be a mom.

THAT EVENING, BARRIE put on her new party dress and styled her hair in a glossy updo. A string of pearls set off the dress's crimson luster, and as she looked at herself in her bedroom mirror, she was glad she'd taken Mallory's advice.

"What do you think, Miley?" she asked, and Miley stared at her silently from his spot on her bed, big eyes fixed on her with that look of adoration she never tired of. "Do I look presentable?"

Barrie turned back to her reflection. She looked pregnant...and in a different way than she was used to viewing this pregnancy. She didn't look scandalously or inconveniently pregnant, but beautifully, roundly, lovingly pregnant. She looked the way she'd imagined she would after she was already married and the pregnancy was planned.

"I look like a success," she murmured.

Funny how big a difference a dress could make—Mallory had been right after all. Barrie leaned closer to the mirror, smoothed on some lipstick and pressed her lips together. Turning to the side, she surveyed the effect with satisfaction. She might like to plan her life down to the last detail, but surprises happened—and this baby was a shock. She might be forced to work under Dr. Berton again, but that didn't mean she'd never set up her own shingle again, either. Barrie couldn't control all of it, but she was still okay.

The snow from earlier had stopped, so the streets were clear when Barrie drove down to the Cruises' place. They lived about fifteen minutes south of Hope on a rural road that gave them a fair amount of privacy. Mallory seemed to have it all—the doting husband, two kids, a cozy house where she loved to entertain... But Mallory had started out with a scandalous pregnancy of her own. She'd only discovered she was pregnant after her boyfriend dumped her for her best friend, and she'd been working a nanny job and trying to hide her growing belly so she could keep her health insurance. Barrie wasn't in the dark about how Mallory's marriage began. Neither of her children were biologically Mike's, and yet they still had a family that gave Barrie a little stab of envy. It was the love in that home, and husband or not, maybe Barrie could give her child something similar. Not every family was traditional.

Barrie parked on the side of the drive, hoping she wouldn't get blocked in. If she got tired, she wanted to be able to leave without too much hassle. The house was lit up with Christmas lights, inside and outside. As Barrie moved up the front walk, she could hear music. Mallory appeared in the window, and she waved, then disappeared again.

"Barrie!" The front door burst open and Mallory shot her a grin. "I'm so glad you made it. Get in here."

Barrie hugged her friend at the front door, and when she came in, Mike was waiting to take her coat. He was dressed down in a pair of khakis and a Christmas sweater, but he was a good-looking guy, and even sweaters that were supposed to be tacky looked good on him.

"Let's see it," Mallory said, standing back.

Barrie felt her cheeks flush, but she took off her jacket and Mallory sighed in contentment. "Mike, she's gorgeous, isn't she?"

"You look great, Barrie," Mike said with a grin.

Katie was dressed in a little golden party dress, and Beau had already managed to get something chocolate smeared on his button-up shirt. The kids came over to give Barrie a hug, and she made the rounds saying hello to the guests who were already there—Mike's partner, Tuck, and his wife, Shana, the youngest two of their four children, and an older couple who were neighbors that lived on the same rural road. She was glad she looked good tonight—she needed this. There was no hiding this pregnancy, so she might as well rock it.

"How are you feeling?" Shana asked. "This is the fun part of pregnancy."

"Fun?" Barrie shook her head. "I'm still adjusting to *being* pregnant."

Shana's eyes glittered as she smiled back. "Enjoy this. You look beautiful, by the way. Mallory's been gushing about this dress, and she was right…wow! You're lucky that the maternity shop opened up. I'm half tempted to have another baby, just so I can shop there! No more catalog maternity shirts for me—"

"Oh, yeah?" Tuck's golden brush of a mustache quivered with humor. "You want to put a fifth one through college?"

Tuck and Shana bantered about the idea of another baby, and while Barrie smiled at their humor, she wasn't in the same position that Shana was in, either. This was harder alone. Mallory caught Barrie's eye across the room, and her friend pointed toward the kitchen.

"I'm just going to see if I can give Mallory a hand," Barrie said, excusing herself. "And if my vote counts, five is a nice round number." She winked at Tuck, who jokingly rolled his eyes, and she crossed the room toward the kitchen, where Mallory waited.

"So, how did lunch with Curtis go?" Mallory asked once they were safely alone. "You didn't call me."

Barrie chuckled. "You were busy getting ready for the party. And it was—" She sighed.

Mallory's expression softened. "Oh, Barrie. I could see the way he looked at you—which is why I threw you at him and ran away. I figured you might have some unfinished business."

"Our business is fifteen years old," Barrie replied. "Some things don't change, and we're both aimed in different directions. My life is here, and he's selling the building I'm leasing and heading out to Wyoming for his own business venture. This is...a pit stop."

"Plans might change," Mallory said.

"Whose?" Barrie spread her hands. "I'm barely holding things together here! I'm not following him anywhere! And as for him, he has nothing to his name besides that building. He has no choice but to sell."

"You aren't mad about it?" Mallory asked with a frown.

"Oh, I'm mad. It's just complicated." Barrie smiled ruefully. "What can I help you with?"

"The cheese platter."

They went to the counter. Mallory pulled some

blocks of cheese from the fridge and passed Barrie a knife. Barrie put her cell phone on the counter and set to work.

"So, was I terrible to leave you with him like that?" Mallory asked.

"No, no…" Barrie opened one of the packages and began to slice. "The thing is, we still have that connection, and I don't know how to describe it. I remember why I fell for him so hard."

"Hmm." Mallory took a different block of cheese and used another knife to slice through the plastic. "How much longer is he here?"

"I don't know. He's leaving after the sale, which has to be finalized Christmas Eve. He offered to teach me how to make those shortbread cookies."

"He knows how?" Mallory asked in surprise.

"He took a class to impress some woman." Barrie shrugged. "And I know it sounds nuts, but learning how to make those cookies like my mom used to make… It would help. I want to be the cookie baker for my child, too. Mom's cookies were…"

They were perfect. They were comforting. They could be whimsical and fun. They were an expression of her love, and of all the traditions that Barrie could pass down from her mom, this one was lodged deep in her heart.

"Are you going to do it?" Mallory looked up.

"I shouldn't." Barrie sighed. "It's a kind offer, but spending time with Curtis is toying with my emotions and I know better than that. We always did have this really strong attraction that overrode our rational thinking. I miss feeling like that—desired, excited… But I'm too old for this crap, Mal."

Mallory laughed and turned back to slicing cheese. "No, you aren't. You're never too old for romance."

"I'm too old to risk it all on a guy I can't trust to follow through," she retorted. "And a baby ups those stakes."

"That is true." Mallory got a platter out of a cupboard, and they started to arrange cheese slices around the edges. "This makes your Christmas a whole lot harder, doesn't it?"

"Yeah," Barrie agreed. "It does."

It reminded Barrie of what she didn't have this Christmas. Her mom, that sense that everything would be okay so long as Gwyneth was there with some timely advice…and Curtis. Every single Christmas since Curtis, she'd felt a little stab of nostalgia for the life she'd wanted so very badly.

"What are you doing this Christmas?" Mallory asked.

"Dinner with my dad," she replied.

"Next Christmas, everything will be different," Mallory said, pointing meaningfully at Barrie's belly.

"I'm glad for that," Barrie confessed. "My baby will be here, and I'll finally have someone to make Christmas for again."

"Again?" Mallory eyed her quizzically.

"Slip of the tongue," she replied. She didn't feel like explaining that one; it would only make Mallory feel sorry for her, and Barrie was tired of pity.

"Christmas with kids is fun," Mallory said. "They

get so excited for Christmas morning, and the little things mean the world to them. Like pancakes for breakfast and decorating cookies… It's for them, really. Not us."

"Well, I'll start seeing Christmas through a child's eyes very soon," Barrie agreed. "And I'm looking forward to it. Nothing will be the same, and I think that's a good thing."

Except Barrie felt like she needed a little Christmas magic in her life. Most of the excitement might be for the kids, but she still needed the warm glow that Christmas brought—the warmth of hearth and home, the hope of love to come. Christmas reminded her of the good in the world, and she wasn't ready to let go of that.

Barrie's cell phone rang, and she put the knife down to answer the call. It was Betty's number.

"Betty?" she said, picking up.

"No, it's me." Curtis's voice was low and close, and she closed her eyes for a moment.

"Hi," she said.

"I'm sorry to interrupt," Curtis said, "but we've got another sick calf. Should I call Dr. Berton and give you the night off?"

"No, no, I'll come." Barrie licked her lips and shot her friend an apologetic look. "How bad is it?"

"I'm not sure this calf will make it," Curtis said. "Just hoping for the best. If you could get here as fast as possible—"

"Yes, I'm on my way." She had rubber boots, an extra farm coat and her vet bag in the back of her truck—she never left home without them. She hung up the phone and Mallory looked at her expectantly.

"Sick calf," Barrie said. "I'm sorry, Mal, but I can't afford to give up any calls to Palmer right now."

"I get it," Mallory replied. "Thanks for coming for a bit, at least. You look amazing."

Barrie chuckled. "Thank you for insisting I buy this dress. You're a good friend."

She gave Mallory a squeeze and then headed toward the living room and the front door. Some new guests were arriving, and Barrie stepped to the side, allowing herself to blend in to the chatter and good humor for a moment.

This was the kind of home that Barrie had been trying to build back when she'd been married to Curtis— the love, the fun, the sense of purpose in being a family. This was the ideal, but it worked only if both partners wanted it more than anything else. Love wasn't enough. That was where she'd gone wrong last time.

"You're leaving already?" Mike said when Barrie reached for her coat.

"Emergency call," she said, holding up her cell phone as if it were proof. "There's a sick calf. I'm sorry. Merry Christmas, Mike."

"You, too, Barrie." Mike helped her get her coat on. "And happy New Year if we don't see you sooner."

Barrie stepped into the winter cold, the chatter and cheery Christmas carols from the party melting into the scene behind her. The sooner this Christmas was over, the better. Life would be a whole lot easier once the pressures of the holidays were past.

Chapter Thirteen

Curtis had transported the calf from the field to the barn, but it hadn't been an easy feat. This was no newborn cow—and a weaned calf couldn't be moved without a cattle trailer. It was weak and had hardly been able to walk from the trailer into the barn, so by the time Curtis had the animal settled, he wasn't sure whether it would pull through or not. He hoped so—he hated it when the cattle suffered.

But Barrie was on her way...

An image of her rose in his mind, but this time it wasn't the young wife with the sparkling eyes. It was the more mature Barrie he'd rediscovered this December. She was still stunning, and stubborn, and capable of tying him up into knots for years to come. Maybe it was because she'd never trusted him to provide for her back when they were married, but he found himself fantasizing about coming back to Hope when he had a financial investment he could stand on, proving he'd been capable and getting her to look at him in a different way. He wanted her respect, but more than that, he wanted her to know she could be safe with him.

The barn door banged shut and he turned to see Barrie coming inside. She passed the stalls and headed down the aisle toward him. This time, it wasn't her pregnancy that took him by surprise, but the party dress she wore under an unzipped winter coat. It swirled around her knees in a silken wave of wine-red material. The top of the dress curved smoothly around her plumped bust, and one porcelain hand rested on the top of her belly, the other carrying her black vet's bag. She walked briskly in a pair of rubber boots—a strange mix with her carefully coifed hair and immaculate makeup, and he couldn't help but grin.

"What's with you and your entrances?" he asked.

A smile curved Barrie's lips. "I was at a party, if you must know."

"Yeah? Is there a distraught date left behind?" he quipped, and as the words came out, he realized that he cared about that detail. A lot.

"Wouldn't you like to know." She stopped when she reached him, her blue gaze meeting his easily. "Which stall?"

Curtis stepped back and she scanned the calf in the stall beside him, her expression sharpening. He could see the professional in her taking over, and he felt mildly in awe of her as she slipped into the stall and put her bag down in the hay. She tucked her dress up underneath her as she crouched to inspect the animal. He couldn't help but wonder if treating sick cattle in party dresses wasn't so unheard of in her world. She worked quickly, checking the calf's temperature and its eyes. She pulled out a syringe and a bottle of medication.

"You were right to get me down here," she said, still facing away from him as she worked. "But I have a feeling this one's a fighter."

"I didn't notice in time," he said.

"It happens." Her tone was distracted, though, and when she finally rose and turned toward him, her expression wasn't reassuring. "Time will tell," she said, answering his unspoken question.

"Yeah." He nodded slowly. Sometimes that's all they could do—wait it out. "Thanks for coming."

"It's my job." That's what she'd told him the first time he'd seen her walk into this barn, but her gaze softened. "You look fantastic, Barrie."

She peeled off her gloves, folding them into an inside out ball. "The gum boots complete the look," she said wryly.

"They kind of do. I don't know...gum boots always suited you."

She leaned against the rail, her gaze fixed on the calf. Then she glanced over at him. "How did you picture yourself at this age, Curtis?"

"You mean back when I was an idealistic kid?" he asked.

"Something like that."

"Well, for one, I was never terribly idealistic," he replied. "But I guess I saw myself as a little more established by the time I was pushing forty. What about you?"

She'd hit her mark, he had no doubt. Look at her— gorgeous, successful in her own career... She was silent for a moment.

"I didn't see any of this," she said quietly. "The baby, the difficulty in running a practice on my own, being alone."

"Well, I guess twenty-year-olds don't tend to look at the practical side of running a veterinary practice," he conceded. "And as for being alone… Barrie, I'm pretty confident that you've got a lineup of admirers."

Barrie shook her head. "I cling to some image I conjured up when I was too young to know what real life was even like. And it's ridiculous—I know that—but I do. I was confident what success looked like back then, and I've arrived in a lot of ways, except it doesn't look the same now that I'm here."

"Your practice, you mean…" He wasn't sure what she was getting at.

"It's more fragile than I thought." She shrugged. "I didn't know how easily I could lose it."

That one stung—would she really lose everything because she had to find a new location for her clinic? He could argue that she wasn't as stable as she'd thought if she was so easily toppled, but this wasn't about defending himself right now.

"I'm sorry, Barrie." He sighed. "How will you do this? I mean, even if your clinic could stay put—what was the plan with the baby?"

Barrie shook her head. "I'm in a tough spot. My dad is still working full-time, and my mom is gone. I'd have to cancel my emergency services, which would be a pretty big hit. I'd need childcare during my regular hours, which can get expensive, but I thought I might be able to sort something out with Mallory. Still, keeping my practice open would be tight."

He could see the glimmer of determination in those blue eyes, though. "You want this bad."

"I've worked for *fifteen years* toward this, Curtis." A tendril had fallen free, and she pushed it away from her cheek. "I dreamed of being a vet as a kid. This isn't just a job, it's a passion." She sighed. "But I never saw myself dropping my newborn off with someone else and walking away for eight hours."

"It's no one's first choice," he agreed.

"I never saw myself as a single mom." She licked her lips.

"You're a planner," he said. "So you're hard on yourself."

"It's more than that," Barrie said. "I wanted to do this the traditional way—be married first, be able to stay home with my kids when they were small. I had a few ideals about starting a family, too, you know."

"Yeah, I remember those." Barrie always had a sense of the right way to do things and the wrong way. His first instincts had invariably fallen on the wrong side of that.

"You aren't the only one who had to juggle a few expectations," Curtis said after a moment. "I'm not exactly proud to be the guy who aged out of bull riding. I wanted to come back to Hope as the conquering success, not the broken-down cowboy."

"You made adjusting your expectations seem a whole lot easier."

"Did I?" He sighed. "Maybe I hid it better."

She looked up, her eyes brimming with sadness, and before he could think better of it, he scooped up her hand in his. She didn't pull away, and he gave her fingers a squeeze.

"Losing you—" He should keep his distance—he knew that—but he found himself leaning closer. "I told myself if I stood firm—" He cleared his throat. "This isn't just residual feelings from back then. You and I—we've got something. Still. Again, maybe. But we've got something."

She pulled her hand back, and his heart sank. Every single day after he'd left, he'd had to talk himself out of calling her, going back… But his pride wouldn't let him. Love her or not, she didn't see him as a man who could protect her, and he hated that. But staying away hadn't allowed him to heal quite so well as he'd hoped, because the minute he saw her again…

"Ever consider working as the vet for a stud farm?" he asked softly.

Barrie shot him a sharp look, then frowned. "Curtis, I'm having a baby."

"I'm sure there would be childcare options in Wyoming, too."

She shook her head. "I need my community now more than ever. I need my dad, too. And he needs me. I can't just up and leave. Besides, if I take a break from my practice, I need to be here to start back up again—stay in people's minds as a valid option in veterinary care."

"I'm asking you to come permanently," he said.

"And if it didn't work between us professionally?"

There she was—all logical and planned out again. She was already putting in a backup plan. It wasn't that he resented her ability to navigate life, but she certainly didn't see a newly purchased stud farm as a viable option for her own career. Good enough for Curtis, maybe, but not for her.

"If you're already looking at making a change—"

"I'm not—not completely." She sighed. "I've worked too hard for what I've got here, Curtis."

"I worked hard, too," he said with a shrug. "But I'm not afraid to face a change."

She licked her lips, and pain flickered deep in her eyes. "You proved that when you left."

"I didn't mean—" he began. "I'm not talking about when we ended things."

She turned away from him and looked at the calf resting in the hay. Curtis would always be the loser who'd walked out on her, wouldn't he? He could go make a raving success of that stud ranch, and if she saw him again, she'd still see the twenty-two-year-old disappointment who hadn't been able to stick it out with her. Maybe he needed to take his own advice and leave Barrie in the past, much as that might hurt. Because some things didn't change, including her distrust.

BARRIE WATCHED THE calf for a couple of beats, her mind spinning. It seemed so easy for him—just change tack! He'd always been flexible that way. If one thing wasn't working, he'd pivot and try something else. Unless his heart was set on it, like bull riding. He'd never given up on that. Too bad that determination couldn't have stretched over to being a husband, too.

She sighed. "I hope it works out for you, Curtis."

"So that's it." His voice was low and resentful.

"What do you want from me?" she demanded, spinning back toward him. "You waltz back into town to sell my building, then offer me some job in Wyoming and get offended when I don't jump? I have a *life*, Curtis!"

"I know." His dark eyes met hers. "And I told you that I'm sorry about this sale. I'm just trying to offer something—"

"A guilt offering. A job. Throwing me a bone." Barrie's voice shook with emotion, and she eyed him resentfully.

"You only need to say no."

But this wasn't about the job offer. She didn't bounce like he did. She didn't pivot when things went wrong. She stuck with it. She dug in her heels. She stayed the course—that was who she was—and while it made life harder in some ways, it meant that the people who loved her could rely on her. Curtis wasn't made of the same stuff. Not when it came to relationships.

He wanted her to just roll with this, but she wasn't the kind of woman who went with the flow very gracefully. She'd tried that rather recently during a convention in Billings. Look where that got her.

"I regret it when I do things spontaneously," she said.

"Like marry me."

"Not everything is about you!" She flung up her hands. "Look at me! Pregnant! I took a chance on a one-night stand because I was lonely… This is where spontaneity got me!"

"So what happened?" Curtis closed the gap between them, his dark gaze drilling down into hers. "Who's the father, Barrie?"

She'd been so determined to keep this secret—take it to the grave if need be—but looking up into Curtis's familiar, brooding face, the secret was too heavy.

"A vet from Billings." The words came out with a bitter taste. "It was our wedding anniversary, and I was at a veterinary convention. I figured if I just kept myself busy that weekend, I wouldn't think about you, but… I met this vet in the bar, and we started talking. I was lonely, and miserable, and remembering how the one guy I'd loved with abandon had abandoned me…and I thought—I need to stop this. I need to take a chance again. So I did. The next morning, I overheard him on a phone call to his wife."

"Did you tell him you were pregnant?"

"Of course. I'm nothing if not proper. I contacted him and he begged me to go away. He was terrified his wife would find out."

"So you did."

"I'd rather do it on my own." She shook her head, tears misting her eyes. She hated this. She hadn't meant to cry—she hadn't exactly made her peace with being a single mom, but she'd very happily turned her back on the cheating louse she'd made the mistake with. She didn't want another woman's husband!

"It was our anniversary," she said, her voice barely

above a whisper. "After fifteen years, you'd think I'd be over you..."

"Barrie..." Curtis slid a hand behind her neck and leaned his forehead down onto hers. She closed her eyes, struggling to get her emotions under control, but as she did, she felt his lips cover hers in a kiss filled with longing. His hands moved from her face down her arms as he stepped closer, his musky scent enveloping her. She'd missed this so much—the way her body reacted to Curtis, melted under his touch. He pulled back.

"It wasn't your fault," he said gruffly.

"Dammit, Curtis, it was!" She stepped back. "I was the idiot who slept with a stranger!"

Her stomach felt cold now that there was space between them, and she ran her hand over her belly protectively. She could accept her mistakes—she didn't need someone to let her off the hook.

"What am I supposed to do?" he demanded. "I can't support you here—"

"I'm not asking you to!" She shook her head, confused. "Why would you do that? This isn't your baby!"

"Because I still love you!" His voice raised to something between a growl and a shout, and she was stunned into silence.

"What?" she whispered.

"I never stopped, Barrie." He heaved a sigh and shut his eyes for a moment. "I... I saw you again, and it was the same as it always was. I can't help it. And spending this time with you just showed me how little has changed. You're the only one who's ever made me feel this way. In fifteen bloody years." His gaze met hers in agonized pleading. "I'd stop if I could…"

"Me, too," she breathed.

"Stop what?" Curtis stepped closer again, his obsidian eyes pinning her to the spot. "Stop what, Barrie?"

"Loving you."

His lips came down onto hers once more, but this time she kissed him back just as hard. Why did Curtis have to come back and upset her careful balance?

"Then let's try again," Curtis said, pulling back.

"How?" She touched her lips, plumped from his kiss.

"Come with me to Wyoming," he said. "We'll start fresh. We'll figure it out."

An impulsive choice—the same kind of impulsive choice that left her pregnant. She wasn't thinking straight right now—she needed reason and logic.

"I can't just leave," she said, shaking her head. "But you could stay here. We lived here once. We could start again—on home soil."

"Except I have nothing here but that commercial building," he replied. "And I can't make enough off your lease to keep myself, let alone the both of us. I can't support you here, Barrie. But I *can* support you in Wyoming. I know you have a hard time trusting that, but if you gave me the chance, I could prove it. I can provide for you and the baby."

And they were right back to the same place they'd been fifteen years ago. He couldn't stay, and she couldn't go.

"It's not the same, Curtis," she whispered. "I'm having a baby. It changes everything…"

"It doesn't have to—"

"It does!" Her voice rose in spite of her attempt to control it. "I can't just leave Hope."

"You can't trust me to take care of you," he concluded.

"I—" Was that it? Maybe. "I need more. I need my home."

Couldn't he understand? Tears welled in her eyes. She'd never loved a man like she'd loved Curtis Porter, but fifteen years hadn't changed enough between them. She had a child to raise and a career to build, and he wanted her to just wing it—hop in a truck with him and see what happened.

She couldn't stand here and do this again. She knew how this ended, and she couldn't think straight—not with him looking at her like that. Not with his body so close, his mouth hovering over hers, waiting for her weakness… She took another step back, trying to find a foundation she could trust.

"I'm not thinking straight. I need some space." Turning away, she picked up her bag and started toward the barn door.

"Barrie, wait—"

"No!" She didn't turn. "I can't do it again, Curtis. Love isn't enough. It never was."

And if she could have broken into a run, she would have. But her pregnancy made that impossible. So she strode toward the door, holding in her tears until she erupted into the frigid night. Hot tears spilled free as she hoisted herself into her truck and turned the key.

Curtis wanted too much. She'd given him everything

she knew how back when they were married, and it hadn't been enough to keep him. All she wanted right now was to get back home to Miley and cry this out.

Tomorrow was Christmas Eve. If she could just get past the holidays, maybe she could find her footing.

Chapter Fourteen

Christmas Eve dawned bright and crisp. Curtis finished his chores and did a check of the livestock in the barn. The calf from last night hadn't made it, and Curtis's already heavy heart felt leaden in his chest.

He kicked the snow off his boots before coming into the mudroom. He could smell fresh coffee percolating in the kitchen and the aroma of fried bacon, but it did nothing to entice him this morning.

"That you?" Betty's voice filtered into the room.

"Yeah."

He hung up his coat and dropped his hat on a peg. Curtis emerged in the kitchen and his aunt gave him a grin.

"Merry Christmas, Curtis."

"It's only Christmas Eve," he said.

"Close enough." She pulled some bacon out of the pan, then shot him a quizzical look. "What's the matter?"

"The calf died last night."

She paused then nodded. "That's too bad. And the others?"

"They recovered," Curtis said. "So no need to call the vet in again."

"Barrie," Betty said. "No need to call Barrie, you mean."

Fine—Barrie. She'd made herself clear last night anyway. If she didn't trust him, then staying here was the right call for her. It was logical—couldn't fault her there, could he? He sighed.

"I need to get this sale finalized and head out, Aunty."

Betty nodded slowly. "And what about Barrie?"

"What about her?" Betty held the plate of bacon toward him and he waved it off. "No, thanks."

Betty cocked her head to one side. "So, just like that?" she demanded. "Off you go—heart in a vise?"

"I have an appointment with Palmer to sign the papers for the sale," he said. "You knew I couldn't stay beyond Christmas."

"I'm not worried about myself," she retorted. "I'll get by. I've got neighbors and…friends."

"Palmer. You can just say it," Curtis snapped, and he was rewarded with a faint blush in his aunt's cheeks.

"He's a friend," she said weakly.

"He's more than that, and you can admit it," he said.

Betty met his gaze with an arch look of her own. "Fine. I'll admit that Palmer and I have gotten close, if you'll admit the same about Barrie."

"Does that help?" Curtis asked. "I'm in love with her still, and the real kicker is that she loves me, too. And it won't work."

"Why not?" Betty frowned. "I've seen the two of you

together lately, and—" Betty shook her head. "There's got to be a way."

"She doesn't trust me." Curtis sighed. "She still doesn't trust me to take care of her, and now she's got a baby on the way and she's determined to stick close to Hope, where she feels in control."

"A baby does change things," Betty said softly.

"So she keeps saying."

But did it have to? He could help her—provide for them. Curtis could be a dad to that child! With Barrie by his side, they'd make that stud farm a success... together. He wasn't asking her to take a back seat, for crying out loud.

"I understand her fear, though," Betty said. "She's had a rough go of it. After you two got divorced, she worked her tail off going to school and supporting herself. There were a few guys who tried to get her attention, but she took your divorce really hard. They didn't really stand much of a chance."

"So it's my own fault," he clarified.

"Curtis, you don't understand." Betty sighed. "The town has been rough on her for this baby. It isn't fair, but you know how people can be. And she's right— she's about to be a mother, and she has to think about everything, not just her heart."

"I want to take her to Wyoming with me. Start fresh."

"And maybe she can't." Betty shook her head. "Why don't you stay here? I could use the help. I can't pay too well, but you'll have room and board. You'd have her. I'm already leaving the ranch to you when I die, but if you and I ran it together in the meantime… There's room for Barrie and the baby here."

"Aunty, I appreciate the offer, but I've got to provide for her properly. I have my pride."

Betty sighed. "Okay. I'm just saying that sometimes, it isn't about who is right and who is wrong—it's about who's going to fix it."

And he'd tried that—did his aunt really think that he hadn't?

"She's not looking for money," Betty said. "That's all."

Curtis rubbed a hand through his hair, then looked out the window for a moment.

"You think she's more worried about me standing by her?" he asked.

"You left her once already," Betty said. "She's about to have a baby, everyone is gossiping about who got her pregnant and she's still clinging to this place. Barrie's never been the materialistic sort. She's holding on because Hope is offering her something she can't refuse."

Something worth more than her pride. Something more than love. Something definitely more than money…

"Some call it control," Betty said. "But maybe she's just holding on for dear life."

The words sent a shudder through him. Was she less in control than she let on?

"You're a wise woman, Betty."

"Glad you noticed." She glanced at her watch. "Are you going to be late to sign those papers?"

Curtis grabbed his hat and pushed it onto his head.

"Do you have any butter?" he asked.

Betty eyed him skeptically. "In the fridge. Why?"

Curtis opened the fridge and pulled out a block. "I'll buy you more."

He headed for the door—he knew what he needed to do. He was going to fix this, once and for all, and if she'd have him, he'd never look back. Hope might be Barrie's safety net, but he intended to be her soft place to fall.

BARRIE STOOD IN front of the mixing bowl, her phone in her hand. She had the ingredients ready to try these shortbread cookies just one more time. She'd cried all night. Poor Miley had done his best to comfort her, and eventually just curled up next to her with his head beside her belly, big eyes fixed on her until she fell asleep, exhausted. She woke up to Miley in the same position.

Her dad had called that morning to wish her a merry Christmas. He was excited about their dinner that evening, and he let slip that he'd bought her some baby things. She'd tried to sound chipper for him, but he wasn't fooled.

"It's Curtis again, isn't it?" her father asked.

"What can I say? He's my weak spot."

"Sweetheart, you'll always have me," her father said quietly. "I'm here to stay, okay?"

"I know, Dad. Thanks."

"And come over early. We'll eat ice cream out of the tub like we used to when you were little."

That was tempting, and she'd agreed. But standing here at the counter, determined to make some edible cookies to go with that ice cream, her heart was aching. Barrie had fallen in love with Curtis again—and she'd known better. The baby squirmed inside her, and she put her hand on her belly. Tears welled in her eyes once more, and she put down her cell phone and covered her mouth with one hand. Why did she have to fall for him like this? Why couldn't her rational mind trump her heart this time around? She'd known where this would go—because it was exactly the same as last time. He wanted her to be different than she was, and she wanted the same of him.

Love wasn't enough.

An engine rumbled into her drive, and Miley barked a few times, ran in a circle through the kitchen, then put his paws on the counter to look out the window. He barked again. Barrie wiped her eyes. It was Christmas—someone was dropping by, and here she was, nursing a broken heart. She didn't want to be seen like this—not now.

"Miley, quiet," she said, but her heart wasn't in it.

She heard boots on the step outside, and then a knock. Miley dropped back to the floor and barked again. She had no choice—she was obviously home. She went to the door and before opening it, she looked out the window. Her heart sped up at the sight of that familiar cowboy hat, bent down to hide Curtis's eyes, but she'd know that jawline anywhere. What was he doing here? Hadn't they done this last night already? With a sigh, she pulled the door open.

"Hey." Curtis stood on the step, and as he glanced up, she could see the lines around his eyes.

"You look tired," she said, stepping back to let him in.

"I didn't sleep," he replied, then planted a block of butter on the counter with a thunk. "Let's get to work."

"What?" She shook her head.

He took off his hat and tossed it next to the butter. As his dark gaze met hers, she felt the tears rise again.

"I missed you," he said, his voice a low rumble.

"Me, too, but it doesn't change anything," she whispered.

"I'm not selling the building," he said. "Your clinic can stay put."

Her heart sped up and she looked at him uncertainly.

"What about your partner?" she asked.

"He can scrape up enough credit on his own, but it means I'm out of the deal."

"But what will *you* do?" she asked, shaking her head.

"I'm staying here," he said. "My aunt still needs help at the ranch, and I'm going to stick around."

"For how long?"

"For good." He brushed a hair away from her face. "Betty pointed something out to me—I've been trying to prove that I could provide for you, but this isn't about finances. This is about something deeper."

"What's that?" she asked, frowning.

"Cookies." Curtis bent down and caught her lips with a quick peck. "We're making some."

Her mind was still reeling with everything he'd just said, and she stared at him, perplexed.

"You made a home for us," Curtis said. "And I never appreciated that. So why should you trust me to appreciate it now?"

"Good point," she whispered.

"Well, I've got a proposal for you. Let's make that home together. You're right—this isn't 1950, and I make a good shortbread. So let's do this together. Let's put together a home, the two of us. I can't promise lots of cash, but I can promise I'll work my heart out to provide."

"So you're really staying…"

He ran his thumb over her bottom lip, then dipped down and kissed her softly. "There are a few things I'm really good at—" his lips curled up suggestively "—and cookies are one of them."

"Curtis, this is all very sweet, but—" The words evaporated on her tongue and his lips covered hers once more. He pulled her in close, and when he'd left her thoroughly breathless, he pulled back.

"I love you," he murmured. "And I want you to trust me, but I understand if you're going to need some time on that. Here's what I want you to do—start a rumor. Tell three people a secret and demand they tell no one."

"What secret?" she asked with a low laugh.

"That I'm the father." He met her gaze evenly.

"But you aren't."

"Don't care," he replied. "Tell them I am. Take away the mystery. Put me on the birth certificate and I'll financially support the both of you. That's how serious I am."

"And then what?"

"Then go out for dinner with me, and let everyone see how I dote on you…" His voice was low and tempting. "Because I'm going to be here, Barrie. I'm not leaving. I don't care how long it takes you to figure out you can trust me again. I'm not giving up."

"You're sure?" she whispered.

"I've never been more sure of anything in my life." He licked his lips. "I want to marry you again, Barrie. I want to raise your child as my own, and I want the whole town to see how happy we are together."

"You'll be running the Porter ranch?" she asked after a moment.

"Yup."

"And you'll be living there?"

"That's the plan."

So close, yet so far away. This house suddenly felt big and rattling. She swallowed. "Is there room for me?"

A grin broke over Curtis's face. "Betty already offered. I'm not asking you to take a back seat, Barrie. I'm asking you to do this with me. Take the time you need with the baby and then start up your practice again. In the meantime, I know we'd sure value your input around the ranch."

She nodded. "Okay, then."

"Yeah?" Curtis bent to catch her eye. "But if you're moving in, I want to marry you."

Barrie chuckled. "So proper."

"To the core." His lips hovered over hers. "I want a home with you. I want matching towels. I want kids who call me Daddy and get mad at me when I'm late. I want to tell people I have to talk to my wife before I agree to something. I want traditions and photo albums and goofy stories that we tell about each other. I want the whole package, Barrie, and for me, that includes the vows. Marry me again. Give me another shot. I'll make it my life's goal to make sure you don't ever regret it."

There would always be risk, but with Curtis, she felt like her heart could start to heal. He was back... but more than that, he'd come home.

"Yes," she said softly. "I'll marry you."

Curtis's lips came down onto hers, and her heart swelled to meet his. She'd never stopped loving him anyway—they might as well make it official.

Epilogue

Barrie lay in the hospital bed, her newborn daughter snuggled in her arms. A girl. She was still in awe... She had a baby girl! Looking down into that tiny face, she felt herself grow. She was a mother, and her life would be devoted to this tiny person for the rest of her days. She could feel it.

Curtis bent down and kissed her forehead, and Barrie raised her gaze to meet his.

"You were amazing," he murmured. "You're like a Viking."

She laughed softly. "I feel like I've been through a battle."

Curtis reached down and ran a finger down their daughter's cheek.

"Do you have a name picked out?" he asked.

"What about Gwyneth, after my mom?" she asked.

"It's perfect." Curtis was silent for a moment. "Can I hold her?"

Barrie shifted the baby into Curtis's arms. He held her awkwardly at first, but the tension started to seep out of his arms as his dark gaze fixed on Gwyneth's tiny, squished face. A smile tickled the corners of his lips, and then his chin trembled. Curtis swallowed hard. He was feeling it, too.

"Wow..." he whispered. "I'm a dad."

"Are we going to be exciting enough for you?" Barrie asked softly. "The domestic life might get a little boring."

"Nah." Curtis touched the baby's cheek with the back of one finger. "This isn't boring... I had fifteen years to chase adventure, and this—" His voice caught. "Babe, this is *everything*."

He sat on the edge of the bed, and Barrie slid a hand over his muscled forearm. She loved him so much, and she'd been afraid that he'd change his mind after his first proposal, but he hadn't. He'd been by her side this whole time, completely in love with her. She hadn't moved in to the ranch house with Betty yet. They were being old-fashioned, and enjoying their engagement a little bit. She'd move in after the wedding made it official. But Barrie had closed her veterinary practice for the short term. As soon as she could handle everything again, she'd reopen.

"So what do you say..." he said quietly. "You ready to set a date for the wedding?"

She nodded. "Yes. I think I am."

Curtis shot her a grin and eased the baby back into her arms. He dipped his head down and caught her lips tenderly with his. The kiss was soft and lingering. When he pulled back, he tucked a tendril of hair behind her ear.

"Good," he whispered. "'Mrs. Porter' always did suit you."

She laughed softly. "Yeah…it did, didn't it?"

Barrie looked back at tiny Gwyneth in her arms. She was so little, so perfect. Her eyes were shut, and her lips were pursed in her sleep… She was theirs. Curtis was right. This was absolutely everything.

* * * * *

If you loved this book,
look for more in Patricia Johns's
HOPE, MONTANA *miniseries:*
THE COWBOY'S CHRISTMAS BRIDE
THE COWBOY'S VALENTINE BRIDE
THE TRIPLETS' COWBOY DADDY
HER COWBOY BOSS
and more.
Available now at Harlequin.com!

COMING NEXT MONTH FROM

H HARLEQUIN®
™

ᏔVestern Romance

Available January 2, 2018

#1673 THE BULL RIDER'S VALENTINE
Mustang Valley • by Cathy McDavid
When Nate Truett and Ronnie Hartman are thrown together
to help with the local rodeo, they are still healing from a
tragic past. Yet an old attraction prevails. Will a Valentine's
Day proposal bring them together for good?

#1674 COWBOY LULLABY
The Boones of Texas • by Sasha Summers
Years ago, cowboy Click Hale broke Tandy Boone's heart.
Now he's her neighbor and a father to a beautiful daughter.
How can Tandy start over with a reminder of everything she
lost living right next door?

#1675 WRANGLING CUPID'S COWBOY
Saddle Ridge, Montana • by Amanda Renee
Rancher and single dad Garrett Slade can't stop thinking
about Delta Grace, the beautiful farrier who works for him.
He's finally ready to take the next step, but he senses she
has a secret...

#1676 THE BULL RIDER'S TWIN TROUBLE
Spring Valley, Texas • by Ali Olson
Bull rider Brock McNeal loves to live on the edge. But when
he starts to fall for Cassie Stanford, a widow with twin boys,
Brock's in a whole different kind of danger!

YOU CAN FIND MORE INFORMATION ON UPCOMING HARLEQUIN® TITLES,
FREE EXCERPTS AND MORE AT WWW.HARLEQUIN.COM.

HWESTCNM1217

Get 2 Free Books,
HARLEQUIN
Western Romance

Plus 2 Free Gifts—
just for trying the
Reader Service!

YES! Please send me 2 FREE Harlequin® Western Romance novels and my 2 FREE gifts (gifts are worth about $10 retail). After receiving them, if I don't wish to receive any more books, I can return the shipping statement marked "cancel." If I don't cancel, I will receive 4 brand-new novels every month and be billed just $4.99 per book in the U.S. or $5.74 per book in Canada. That's a savings of at least 12% off the cover price! It's quite a bargain! Shipping and handling is just 50¢ per book in the U.S. and 75¢ per book in Canada.* I understand that accepting the 2 free books and gifts places me under no obligation to buy anything. I can always return a shipment and cancel at any time. Even if I never buy another book, the two free books and gifts are mine to keep forever.

154/354 HDN GLPV

Name _____ (PLEASE PRINT)

Address _____ Apt. #

City _____ State/Prov. _____ Zip/Postal Code

Signature (if under 18, a parent or guardian must sign)

Mail to the **Reader Service:**
IN U.S.A.: P.O. Box 1867, Buffalo, NY 14240-1867
IN CANADA: P.O. Box 611, Fort Erie, Ontario L2A 9Z9

Want to try two free books from another line?
Call 1-800-873-8635 or visit www.ReaderService.com.

*Terms and prices subject to change without notice. Prices do not include applicable taxes. Sales tax applicable in N.Y. Canadian residents will be charged applicable taxes. Offer not valid in Quebec. This offer is limited to one order per household. Books received may not be as shown. Not valid for current subscribers to Harlequin Western Romance books. All orders subject to credit approval. Credit or debit balances in a customer's account(s) may be offset by any other outstanding balance owed by or to the customer. Please allow 4 to 6 weeks for delivery. Offer available while quantities last.

Your Privacy—The Reader Service is committed to protecting your privacy. Our Privacy Policy is available online at www.ReaderService.com or upon request from the Reader Service.

We make a portion of our mailing list available to reputable third parties that offer products we believe may interest you. If you prefer that we not exchange your name with third parties, or if you wish to clarify or modify your communication preferences, please visit us at www. ReaderService.com/consumerschoice or write to us at Reader Service Preference Service, P.O. Box 9062, Buffalo, NY 14240-9062. Include your complete name and address.

SPECIAL EXCERPT FROM

H HARLEQUIN®

Western Romance

Rodeo cowboy Brock McNeal doesn't date women with kids. So why can't he stop thinking about single-mom Cassie Stanford?

Read on for a sneak preview of
THE BULL RIDER'S TWIN TROUBLE,
the first book in Ali Olson's
SPRING VALLEY, TEXAS *series!*

Brock hurried up the steps to the front porch, noting the squeaking of the stairs and the flaking white paint.

He hoped the widow didn't expect him to be working there too often. If his mother was so desperate to have him around, why would she give him a big job that might eat into all the time he had at home?

Brock brushed the question aside and knocked. He'd go through a short introduction and make his way back for his hot meal, then he'd begin preparing for his next rodeo.

After a few seconds, the door opened and any thought of food or rodeos disappeared. He stared, caught off guard by the lovely woman who stood there.

Her dark brown hair fell around her shoulders in a mass of curls, framing an open, sweet face and lips that promised more than just smiles for the guy lucky enough to get to kiss them.

Brock suddenly felt like an awkward teenager. It took all his effort to arrange his face into a cool, confident smile. "Hello, ma'am," he said, putting on a slightly thicker drawl than usual. "I'm Brock McNeal. My folks live just over the way. They said Mrs. Stanford was in need of some help fixin' up this place, and I thought it best to come introduce myself."

A plan was already formulating in Brock's mind. Make nice to the old lady, get in good with the beautiful mystery woman, then ask her for a date. Easy enough.

The woman smiled. "Nice to meet you. Call me Cassie. Your mother was so sweet to offer your help."

Brock's mind shifted gears quickly. The widow was Cassie.

Before he could say anything, two young boys shot into the doorway, their identical faces peering at him from behind Cassie's legs.

"Zach, Carter, say hello to Mr. McNeal. He'll be helping us fix up the place a bit."

Brock tried his hardest to keep the disappointment off his face, but he wasn't sure he succeeded.

Of course she had kids. There had to be something or his mother would've just come out and told him about her sneaky little plan. She knew well enough by now he didn't plan on having any children, and that meant no dating women with kids, either.

Don't miss THE BULL RIDER'S TWIN TROUBLE
by Ali Olson, available January 2018
wherever Harlequin® Western Romance books
and ebooks are sold.

www.Harlequin.com

Copyright © 2018 Mary Olson

Looking for more satisfying love stories
with community and family at their core?

**Check out Harlequin® Special Edition
and Harlequin® Western Romance books!**

New books available every month!

CONNECT WITH US AT:

Harlequin.com/Community

 Facebook.com/HarlequinBooks

 Twitter.com/HarlequinBooks

 Instagram.com/HarlequinBooks

 Pinterest.com/HarlequinBooks

ReaderService.com

**ROMANCE WHEN
YOU NEED IT**

HFGENRE2017R

THE WORLD IS BETTER WITH

Romance

Harlequin has everything from contemporary, passionate and heartwarming to suspenseful and inspirational stories.

Whatever your mood, we have a romance just for you!

Connect with us to find your next great read, special offers and more.

/HarlequinBooks

@HarlequinBooks

www.HarlequinBlog.com

www.Harlequin.com/Newsletters

HARLEQUIN®

A *Romance* FOR EVERY MOOD™

www.Harlequin.com

SERIESHALOAD2015

LOVE
Harlequin
romance?

Join our Harlequin community to share your thoughts and connect with other romance readers!

Be the first to find out about promotions, news, and exclusive content!

Sign up for the Harlequin e-newsletter and download a free book from any series at

www.TryHarlequin.com

CONNECT WITH US AT:

Harlequin.com/Community

 Facebook.com/HarlequinBooks

 Twitter.com/HarlequinBooks

 Instagram.com/HarlequinBooks

 Pinterest.com/HarlequinBooks

ReaderService.com

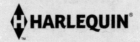

**ROMANCE WHEN
YOU NEED IT**

HSOCIAL2017